CONCH REPUBLIC

1828

KEY WEST

Look for other Adventure & Western novels by
Eric H. Heisner

Africa Tusk

Wings of the Pirate

West to Bravo

Seven Fingers a' Brazos

T. H. Elkman

Short Western Tales: Friend of the Devil

Follow book releases and film productions at:
www.leandogproductions.com

Conch Republic
Island Stepping with Hemingway

Eric H. Heisner

Illustrations by Emily Jean Mitchell

Copyright 2019 by Eric H. Heisner

Visit our website at
www.leandogproductions.com

Illustrations by: Emily Jean Mitchell
Contact: **mlemitche@gmail.com**
Website: www.mlemitchellart.com

Dustcover jacket design: Clint A. Beach
Contact info: Thebeachboy72@gmail.com

Edited by: Story Perfect Editing Services

Hardcover ISBN: 978-0-9995602-4-2

Printed in the United States of America

Dedication

For Aunt Joan –
who never discouraged me from dreaming,
always cheered me on,
never encouraged me to have a real job,
and showed me to never give up.

Special Thanks

Amber W. Heisner,
Clint Beach, Emily Jean Mitchell,
& Billie Beach Jr.

Note from Author

There is something very special about the Florida Keys and that place at the end of the road, Key West in particular. A few years after graduating film school in Chicago, I had just completed a television production job and found myself at a crossroads. A romantic relationship had just come to an end, and the close group of friends I shared an apartment with was going their separate ways. My personal possessions went into storage in my parent's basement and it was a rare time in life when I had some unfilled time on my hands until my next job.

Having a passion for flying boats, seaplanes and the history of the Caribbean, I packed my truck with a backpack of clothes, my guitar and a bicycle strapped to the pickup topper and headed south. My first objective was to charter a water takeoff and landing with Chalk's Ocean Airways, from Miami, on a Grumman Mallard seaplane to the Bahamas. Being on a tight budget, I only stayed in Bimini a short while before heading back to my home on wheels.

The next two months I spent exploring the set of islands that extend to the southernmost tip of the United States while living a vagabond lifestyle in my pickup truck. As with most journeys in life, the adventures would never need to be repeated, but experiencing island time in Key West gave me a great love of *The Conch Republic*.

Eric H. Heisner

April 23rd, 2019

Imagination is like a magic hat ... unless you put something in, nothing comes out.

Ernest Hemingway lived and enjoyed life in the Florida Keys for twelve years beginning in 1928. He wrote several classic stories in Key West such as *Death in the Afternoon, Green Hills of Africa*, and *To Have and Have Not*. Many writers have used the islands as their muse, but he lived it to the fullest …

I

At the western end of the island, a chattering crowd of tourists assemble at the waterfront pier as the sun begins to set over the Gulf of Mexico. Mallory Square is filled with sightseers and street-entertainers that intermingle, while watching lazing sailboats drift in the calm breeze across a watery horizon. A vacationer, sweat glistening on freshly, sunbaked skin, walks by with a newly purchased tropical shirt and a cell phone held up against his ear.

Despite the elevated level of crowd noise from the assembly of people around him, he speaks into the handheld telephone device. "Hello, is Moselly there?" He takes the cellular phone away from his ear, looks at the glowing screen a moment to make sure he is connected and then presses the device to the side of his head again.

"This is Jon Springer... Hello?"

Eric H. Heisner

Jostled in the midst of the energetic sunset gathering, it doesn't seem like the best place to attempt a phone call. Despite the noise around him, he continues to speak into the cell phone. "Yes... I did notice that you're new in the office." Jon moves nearer to an inventive unicyclist elevated on his six-foot custom perch, juggling fiery torches while a young blonde-haired boy stands below readied with a pail of water. He looks to the street-performer, high up on the specially modified single-wheel apparatus, tossing flaming batons skyward. He then glances down at the young child holding the bucket of water. "What's he gonna do with that?"

The garrulous street performer continues to tread back and forth on the unicycle pedals, as he catches up his flaming torches in one hand and motions for the young boy to raise the water bucket higher. One by one, the gifted entertainer on the jury-rigged unicycle twirls the flame-tipped batons into the small bucket of water to the amazement and joy of the gathered audience. Relieved, Jon sighs, "Ahh, a land of no lawyers."

~*~

In a dimly lit warehouse with blacked-out windows, a primitive boxing ring is set up in the center of the open area. The sharp clang of a fight-bell rings and two pugilists step from opposite corners, where sagging lengths of nautical rope wrap around four-by-four posts. The single lamp, high above the stage, casts the fighters' features in shadow.

One of the boxers steps forward and provocatively jabs out the padded glove on his right fist. The circling opponent responds with a tap from his own glove and hooks a roundhouse swing, a miss to its intended target. The two combatants hop away from the other and continue the circling dance, while several dozen onlookers stand in the shadows around the boxing ring placing money wagers.

Island Stepping with Hemingway

~*~

At the outdoor gathering in Mallory Square, the nearly inaudible voice of the office receptionist returns at the other end of the cellular phone call. Jon turns away from the noisy crowd and responds with a sharp tone of growing annoyance. "Just tell him that his client, *J.T. Springs* is on the line." Working his way through the clusters of vacationing people gathered for the evening sunset, Jon gazes around and seems to be enjoying the festive chaos of the nightly celebration.

A successful paperback mystery and adventure writer, Jonathan Tyler Springer, alias 'J.T. Springs' is in his middle years, traveling to the one-time literary island-mecca of Key West to gain inspiration. Jon stumbles into the hind-end of a plump tourist woman in a flowing, red-flowered sundress and she gives him a glare over her enormous wide-frame sunglasses. He still holds the phone to his ear and smiles apologetically. "Sorry, Ma'am... Excuse me."

The office receptionist on the other end of the telephone line replies to his apology and he responds, "No, not you... Yes, I'm still here on the phone waiting." Perturbed, Jon shakes his head and smiles kindly at the attentive female tourist. "That's correct. Tell him J.T. Springs is still on the line for him." He continues to keep the cellular phone pressed to his ear as he weaves slowly through the boisterous crowd who pose and snap souvenir photographs of the picturesque evening event. "I can't come into the office. Tell him I'm still in Key West."

There is a probing tap on his shoulder and Jon turns around to find the oversized, floral print-dressed woman facing him with a bizarre look of recognition on her features. She lowers her wide-rimmed sunshades a bit and peers over them to reveal distinct lines of a raccoon-mask sunburn pattern surrounding her eyes and connecting over her nose.

She peels back her round cheeks to smile pleasantly and utter, "Are you the adventure/mystery writer, J.T. Springs?"

Jon glances down at the female admirer and offers a slight, affirming nod. His attention returns to his phone call, as the receptionist finally connects him with the Los Angeles writing agent, C. Moselly. The fast-talking, nasally voice of the big city literary representative chimes in. "Who's that there? Who's on the line?"

"Hello Moselly, its Jon." The agent's voice on the other end of the call becomes distant as if responding to someone else in the room. "Yes, we have to have lots of monkeys there! It's a book about the jungle, sweetheart." Jon takes the cell phone from his ear and looks at it strangely before he brings it back to listen again. He glances over and notices the flower-patterned tourist woman still watching him admiringly. Turning away from her, Jon speaks into the phone, "Moselly? Are you talking to me?"

"Yeah, Jonny boy, be right with you... Yes, yes, yes! That'd be great if you could get a tiger too, and don't get any of those cheap monkeys either. I want big ones... Gorillas?

Out of the corner of his eye, Jon notices the tourist woman still gawking at him, and he forces a grin as he turns into the crowd with the phone at his ear. He continues to listen to the agent's one-sided conversation on the other end of the phone call. "Whatever you call them, make them big. Yeah, yeah, real big... King Kong size would be about right. How much is that gonna cost us?"

"Hello, Moselly?"

"Okay ... Jon, you still there? Yeah, yeah... Okay fine, the big orange fuzzy ones like Clint Eastwood gets."

The admiring tourist woman grabs a firm hold of Jon's elbow and pulls herself uncomfortably close. She speaks above the din of the gathered crowd in a rasping whisper

Island Stepping with Hemingway

"I've read almost all of your recent books." Jon looks down at her chubby, sun-pinked fingers wrapped around his arm. "Thanks, I really appreciate it." His attention is returned to the phone call as Moselly speaks up. "Jon, is that you?"

"Yeah, Moselly. I'm still here."

The female fan gives Jon's arm a strong tug and stands on her sandaled toes to speak loudly in Jon's available ear. "Your books are right up there with Louis L'Amour and Danielle Steele. I love them!" She clutches Jon tighter and breathes heavy as she speaks. "They're always easy to follow, and small enough to fit in my purse so I can just pull them out anywhere." Excited spittle flies from her lips as she speaks. "They are wonderful little reads whenever I pick one up at the airport or discount book-bin."

Jon feigns a friendly smile for the admiring fan and returns his attention to the phone call as Moselly continues. "The new book is great; everyone loves it! It's a gold mine and will make a great film." The clicking sounds of buttons on a calculator are heard as Moselly tallies up sales numbers. "Where are you and who is that talking to you over there?"

Jon tries to weave through the crowd to lose the attentive woman but she doggedly clutches at his free arm. The persistent follower is getting very clingy and bothersome. She strains to overhear Jon's phone conversation and keeps nudging herself flirtatiously closer while unabashedly declaring, "I thought you'd be much, much older. My ninety-three year-old mother loves your audiobooks too."

Jon finally tugs his arm loose from her sweating grasp and tries to maneuver away. "Thanks… I'm on the phone."

Moselly pipes up through the earpiece on the cellular phone. "You're getting hard to hear pal. Why don't you come on into the office so we can talk?"

"I'm still in Key West."

"Well, get your butt back here. I'm planning the exposition of your newest volume. You really need to start making appearances at these premiere events."

~*~

The two fighters in the poorly lit arena grapple and split away from the other. The small surrounding crowd cheers and grumbles as jabbing leather boxing mitts splatter against sweated torsos. The less-muscled boxer eases back along the ringside and turns an ear to a long-haired, scruffy adviser who hangs from the roped-off corner.

He confirms with a nod and continues the circling dance with his much younger opponent. In a flash, a series of punches whirl out and the exchange of fists put both men against the ropes. After a brief pause, they come at another again and the mature fighter connects a deflected jab to the opponent's shoulder and an uppercut to the ribs.

~*~

Jon maneuvers through the gathering of sightseers and looks behind to see the female fan tenaciously pursuing him. He switches the cell phone to his other ear and continues speaking to his literary agent. "They're too embarrassing..." Moselly's shrill voice on the other end of the line cuts Jon off. "Your domestic and international book sales could be twice as much if the public could see your good-looking mug and not just hear of some faceless *J.T. Springs* fella. Look at Lee Child or that horror guy, King!" The slurping sound of Moselly drinking from a coffee cup is followed by a choking cough. "Well, not King so much. We could even hire someone to pose and look like you, or better, whatever you want to look like! We can make you up with a mustache, muscles, whatever..."

The pursuing tourist woman starts to perspire and breathes heavily as she finally catches up to Jon and ogles him over her oversized sunglass frames. "I thought you'd have some big scars... or bullet holes maybe?" Jon gives her an odd look and tries to ignore her continued presence as he speaks to Moselly on the phone. "The book takes place in Africa."

Moselly's voice chirps on the phone line. "Your point?"

"You'll have Indian tigers and orangutans running around with waiters in Tarzan pants and coconut bras."

"I could try to get an elephant."

"With big ears or little?"

"Does it matter?"

Jon wobbles his head, disgusted at his oblivious agent, as he tries to move through the mass of people gathered for the nightly sunset celebration. "Forget it, Moselly."

"You're not going to show at this one?"

"No."

The office intercom buzzes at Moselly's desk, and he answers it while still on the phone-line with Jon. "What is it?" The receptionist's voice crackles over the office intercom. "Clark is on line two."

"Alright, I will be right with him."

Jon listens to Moselly's multi-tasking a moment then finally blurts out the intended meaning of his telephone call. "I'm not coming back to Los Angeles."

"We could do the launch in New York."

"I'm not doing any of it anymore."

"Hold on a minute! What are you talking about?" Moselly shifts the telephone receiver to his other ear and speaks directly into the intercom speaker on his office desk. "Not you, dammit... Put Clark on hold." The agent pushes several buttons on the intercom and speaks into the phone, "When was it you were getting back to L.A.?"

Jon responds, "I'm staying down here for a while."

Moselly spins his high, leather chair away from the flashing desk intercom and cradles the phone on his shoulder as he addresses Jon. "Are you having those fanciful delusions of being Ernest Hemingway or that guy Alan Shepard again?"

"Do you mean Sam Shepard?

"What?"

"The author and playwright, not the astronaut."

"Whatever…"

Jon looks to the setting sun on the watery horizon, feeling the warm glow and the joyous electricity of the crowd. "No more of these cheap mystery or high-adventure novels. I'm pulling out to write something serious." Moselly slaps his open palm on the armrest and winces as he shakes off the painful tingle in his fingers and hand. "Serious writing doesn't make any money! Your types of books make lots of money. They've made *you* a crap-ton of money. You can't disappear to Key where? Mexico, that's crazy!" Moselly's desk intercom buzzes again. "Clark is now on line four."

The literary agent spins his chair and stabs his finger at the base of his desk intercom. Several buttons flash and click as they connect and disconnect. "Tell him I'll call right back. No, get him on the line again. What will you do for income?" Jon starts to get confused as to who Moselly is speaking to, but responds anyway, "I'll get along fine for a while."

Moselly's voice comes through on the telephone line, loud and clear. "Have you gone totally insane? Too many Rum Punches! We talked about this before… You're hot now! This is your prime time to milk it with everything you've got. Who knows what could happen if you take a long vacation?"

Jon stands with the festive crowd, facing the orange glow of the setting sun on the horizon. "This is not a vacation. I'm finished writing those kinds of stories for good."

He can hear Moselly creaking in his chair and frantically thumbing through his desktop rolodex as the agent continues to speak, "You can't be serious. I know a good

Island Stepping with Hemingway

doctor you can talk to. He's got pills or something for this sort of thing and helped Carrie Fisher several times."

The tourist lady-fan has moved in close at Jon's side again and talks loudly at his other ear. "How do you ever come up with all those exotic locations and amazing stories?"

He looks at her and shrugs. "I make 'em up."

Moselly's voice is again chirping on the cellular phone. "You can't just stop writing them. That's not how it's done. This is your biggest book yet!"

Jon looks at the exuberant tourist woman still gawking at him adoringly as he speaks to Moselly, "Send me a check." He hands over the cellular phone with the glowing screen to the female fan and smiles graciously. "Hollywood is calling... It's for you."

The woman is clearly overjoyed as she takes the electronic device from the popular novelist. She looks at the phone a moment, peels her plump, rosy cheeks back to a wide grin, and then puts the phone to her ear. "Hello Darling..."

Jon turns away as the orb of sun finally dips below the horizon and the crowd erupts in cheers and applause.

~*~

Inside the boxing ring, the combatants duke it out with sweat dripping from their shadowed features. One of the fighters pauses to consult with his ringside advisor again. From the corner of his eye, he sees, too late, a glove come at his head, as the swinging roundhouse punch connects with a smacking blow which spins him to the canvas matt.

The crowd hushes as the younger, muscle-gleaming fighter dances a victorious circle around the fallen opponent. The long-haired consultant outside the ring slaps his hand on the ring floor and lowers his forehead to the sagging rope. Several fistfuls of cash are exchanged as the sunlit cracks along the warehouse walls slowly fade to black.

II

The island streets of Key West are warm and sunny, with the historic lighthouse at the western end jutting skyward from the lush tree canopy. Tourist shops along Duval Street put out a variety of displayed goods that range from t-shirts and trinkets to transvestite apparel. The new day sunshine heats the freshly washed puddles along the street into steam, cleansing away the revelry of the night prior.

In running shorts and a sweaty t-shirt, Jon jogs south along the main drag, passing a second-hand bookshop with a propped up display of novels out front. He spots several of his own paperback mystery-adventure novel titles under the author moniker of *J.T. Springs*. His movie poster styled book-cover names range from: *African Tuskers, West of the Rio Bravo, Tale of a Cowboy* and *Pirated Wings*. He slows his running pace as he trots by and raises an eyebrow at the hand painted sign out front which reads: *Pirates, Cowboys & Outlaws welcome here! Enjoy the mystery & colorful adventure stories of J.T. Springs.*

Heaving a grunt and swiping the drips of sweat from his temples, Jon turns away and continues his running pace. He strides past the high brick wall surrounding the museum and Hemingway house, on toward the landmark for the Southernmost Point of the United States. Ahead, the cone shaped beacon reads: *The Conch Republic – 90 miles to Cuba.* Skirting the colorfully ringed beacon, Jon looks out to the open waters as sailing vessels and fishing boats move out in the flat, calm blue ocean.

The throaty rumble of dual, radial airplane engines is heard and Jon watches a high-winged, amphibious seaplane skims over the swells like a powerboat about to take flight. Finally leaping into the sky, a watery mist of clinging ocean spray trails from the flying ship's boat hull and tail section. The chartered aircraft soars into the western horizon toward the scattered islands of the Dry Tortugas.

Pushing back the constant drip of sweat from his brow, Jon continues his morning run down the wide, crushed coral beach. The coarse white sand crunches with every running stride, while the rising tide caressed the shore with a gentle lapping of incoming waves. Wide rings of sweat darken his shirt as the rising sun begins to warm the thick, salty breeze.

At the far end of the shoreline, the beach narrows away near the quaint site of Key West International Airport. Leaping the sidewalk, Jon crosses the roadway and cuts inland through palm frond-lined neighborhoods of bungalow style shacks and curious looking "eyebrow"-roofed houses. Jon moves at a deliberate pace down the residential street and lets thoughts and worries of his professional future slip away, as a serene outlook of island life cleanses his mind and soul.

~*~

Island Stepping with Hemingway

On a small avenue, a few blocks from the main tourist route through Old Town, a tall foliage-formed fence encloses an elegant island estate. The preserved, turn of the century home is wrapped with colorfully painted wooden porches, trimmed by elaborate twisted metal railings and lush gardens. Shirt sweated through, pausing fleetingly to catch his breath, Jon enters the front wrought iron gate and trots the pathway around behind the main house to the two story structure, formerly known as a carriage house.

A spiraling set of rusted stairs lead up to a narrow balcony and private apartment residence over the garage. Pausing at the base of the stairway, Jon does some brief cool-down stretches, as he gazes to the well-tended gardens and overhanging canopy of vegetation. He listens to the flitting birds in the trees chatter and call out the sounds of an island morning coming to life. Finally, he climbs the metal stairs to the balcony and enters the apartment, letting the spring-hinged screen door creak shut behind him.

~*~

The island of Key West comes alive with a steady drone of motor scooters weaving through and around the stacked streets of cars and bicycles. A kitschy tourist shuttle named *The Conch Train* rolls down the avenue clanging a bell, with the loudspeaker narrating local island attractions and history. Catering to the day-tripper trade, stores open and shopfront displays are put out to the sidewalks, as sunshine brings life and prosperity to the final landmass in the chain of Keys.

~*~

The sound of running water in the apartment shower turns off, and Jon, in a pair of khaki shorts, comes out from the steamy bathroom, mopping his wet hair with a towel. He moves across the room and weaves around a driftwood constructed coffee table and other 'island rustic' furnishings.

A scuff-sided, leather suitcase sits unfolded on a cane-back chair, and Jon reaches inside to pull out a fresh shirt.

On the opposite wall atop a chest level bookcase sits a vintage model Royal Quiet de Luxe typewriter and a stack of ivory-colored writing paper with sun-tinted edges. Beside the shelved display of leather bound volumes stands a carved-leg table and matching set of chairs to serve as a provisional desk. Atop the dark polished wooden surface, a tattered mailbag style briefcase lies next to a portable laptop computer.

Jon tosses the wet bathing towel over a rattan armchair and stands before his modern, electronic writing machine. Glancing at the stack of paper beside the classic typewriter, Jon earnestly considers it a moment, then opens the folded-over screen of the computer and touches the power-on button. As the slim laptop device begins to hum through the startup process, Jon draws back the chair and sits contented, as the lit screen flashes a stock photo of a tropical paradise.

With a series of taps on the finger-touch control pad, the colorful island image swaps for a stark white screen with a blinking pulse of a black cursor at the top of the blank page. Feeling invigorated by a newfound sense of creative freedom, Jon's nimble hands blaze away at the illuminated keyboard. His fingertips flurry through a succession of keystrokes in an outpouring of inspiration, then pause and click away again.

Another brief spurt of imagination forms dark lines of words across the computer screen until Jon halts his typing hands, keeping them poised above the keyboard. During the long tentative pause, fingers dance in the air to an empty spell. Jon stares at the white screen as his palms hover in the void, not touching the keyboard, waiting for further motivation. Finally, heaving a disheartened sigh, he sits back in the chair, looks out the window to the clear blue tropical skies over the treetops and folds his arms across his chest.

III

Sometime later... Jon remains staring blankly at the pulsing black cursor on the mostly empty computer screen. The blank page awaits, but the fingers fail to motivate on the panel of lettered keys. The sharp, piercing bell-ring of an antiquated telephone breaks him from his somber trance.

Jon gazes around the room for the source of the sound. He moves from his writing spot to an old-fashioned telephone on a side-table at the end of the sofa. The shrill bell-ringing reverberates as Jon stares at the vintage rotary phone, and then instinctively looks to the vacant spot near his wallet where his cell phone once was.

Lifting the telephone's handset from the base cradle, Jon hesitantly holds it to his ear. "Hello... Can I help you?" Silence ensues, and he takes the receiver handle away from the side of his face, looking at the ear and mouth components. From faraway, a faint crackling voice can be heard on the end of the line and Jon holds the old telephone back to his ear. "Yes, this *is* Jon Springer. And who is *this*?"

Suddenly a welcoming smile of recognition beams across Jon's features as he replies, "How did you find me, you ol' sea dog and where did you get this phone number?" Jon listens a moment and responds, "Yeah, I guess it is sort of a start to a new life." He grins and turns to look around the small garage apartment before replying again. "I ditched my personal cell phone yesterday somewhere in Mallory Square. Who knew there was even a working phone in this place?"

Jon lifts the bulky telephone base from the side table and carries it across the room with the phone cord trailing. Looking out the front glass windows to the lush gardens surrounding the main house, he nods in reply to the caller. "You're right, it is an island... I'm just doing some writing." Jon shakes his head. "No, not another one of those potboilers... I don't think I'll even let it get released in paperback." A cheerful smile stretches across Jon's features as he strolls around the small apartment holding the old rotary telephone at his side. "What was that? You're sailing down here today? Yeah, I really need to settle in a bit and get some writing done... You're already on the boat?"

Moving over to an aged, leather club chair, Jon sits on the padded armrest and puts the telephone base to his lap. "Conch Republic Tavern... Okay, it's a place in Old Town? Yeah, it's just a just a few streets over." Jon casually brushes his fingers through his still damp hair and beams happily "Alright, see you at the Conch Republic for drinks at eleven." The call disconnects and Jon nests the phone handle on the base cradle and looks at the vintage contraption on his knee He puts it aside on the table, gathers the cord to tuck away and shakes his head with a pleased grin. "Scott Fulton.. Interesting times always around the corner with that guy."

Island Stepping with Hemingway

~*~

A gleaming white sailing yacht bobs in blue waters as it slices through the ocean waves. The stretched canvas on the main mast begins to flutter as the wind shifts directions. Dressed in elite mariner garb like an Abercrombie model, Scott Fulton lowers the satellite telephone from his ear, pushes a button to clear the small display screen and then holds it at his side. His daring, yet dubious, eyes watch the skyline as a dark, mysterious-looking vessel powers in the direction of his cruising sailboat.

Fulton continues to watch the horizon as he adjusts the lines on the canvas in an attempt to capture the faltering wind. The yacht's idling sails fall limp around the main mast as the hull rocks and sways with the rolling of the ocean swells. Turning the rudder wheel, Fulton's enquiring gaze narrows as the foreign boat cruises ever nearer. "Oh, shit..."

Stuck in the doldrums, the wind-challenged sailboat drifts aimless as the yards of sail canvas sag on the lines. Fulton watches the intimidating, sleek black yacht as it cuts the engines and eases alongside his ineffective sailing vessel. Two professional-looking ship crewmen appear and toss grappling hooks across to the wooden deck of Fulton's boat. The lone occupant on the sailboat hollers over to the yacht. "Hey, watch it fellas! I just had those rails refinished."

Disregarding the aggravated plea, the crewmen pull the two water-crafts together and lash the joining lines tight. The ship captain of the military-looking yacht appears on the upper deck and leans on the rail with a subdued demeanor. He wears a pair of dark-tinted sunshades and a gray, combat-style life vest over some sort of informal naval uniform.

Fulton looks up at the commanding figure and feigns a kindly salute with the satellite phone, as he moves his other hand around to his back. He calls out to the ship's captain,

"Ahoy, Longley. I already told you I would replace that lost cargo and pay the money when I could." Fulton swallows a gulp of air and attempts to maintain his calm assertiveness. "This intimidation crap on the high seas is bad business."

Several more stone-faced crewmen appear on the deck of the adjacent yacht and stare down at him. Fulton mutters under his breath, "Damn pirates..." Suddenly, in a flash, he swings a pistol from behind his back and fires a shot to the figure at the rail in the combat life vest. The unexpected gunshot hits the ship captain low center and spins him to the deck, out of sight. In an instant, a dozen more armed crewmen appear on the foredeck and the rattling click of machine gun parts disrupts the peace of the open ocean.

Fulton looks up to see the yacht's mercenary pirate crew taking aim at him, and he drops his fired handgun to the wooden planks of the sailboat deck. "Ah, hell. I'm screwed." The pistol clatters at his feet and he promptly kicks it aside. Still gripping the satellite telephone in his other hand, Fulton presses the redial button before he lifts his arms skyward. "Hold it fellas… I surrender."

IV

Inside the carriage house apartment, Jon shuffles through the drawers of the small kitchenette and scans around the room. Coming up empty handed, he mutters aloud, "Hmm, aren't there any keys for this place?" The sound of the telephone bell ringing again distracts him from his hunt, and Jon looks at the old rotary device with interest before finally lifting the handset to answer it. "Hello...?"

A soured look of disappointment comes over Jon's features when he recognizes the familiar voice of his agent. "Yeah, Moselly, it's me... I'm just as surprised as you are." Holding the phone, he continues his search of the apartment. "I moved in yesterday. How did you even get this number?" Jon walks the perimeter of the small apartment, still looking for a house key. "No... Yes, I wasn't kidding. I've got to run. Not a jog... I've got a meeting with someone."

The literary agent's chatter on the other end of the phone line starts to protest excitedly and Jon cuts him off. "Yes, it is someone important... No, it's nothing like that." Irritated, Jon clenches his jaw as he holds the phone to his ear. "Nobody knows what I'm writing next. I'll talk to you later." Jon hangs up the old telephone in a huff and sets it on the edge of the writing table.

After a final glance around the apartment for a key to the front entry, Jon steps out and pulls the door shut behind. He lets the outside screen door spring closed and trots down the spiral stairway to the gardens below. The distinct sound of the phone ringing again can be heard from the apartment. Halfway past the main house, Jon hesitates for a moment, shakes his head disgusted and continues on to the street.

Just outside the front gate, an index card-sized paper flyer skitters across the sidewalk and Jon puts his foot on it. He lifts it from the pavement and reads the caption under a pencil sketch of a set of boxing mitts.

Be there Ringside!
See the grandson of a legendary boxing trainer who
sparred with Hemingway and continues the tradition.

After reading the message, Jon turns it over to the backside. He stares at the blank flip-side of the flyer then folds it and tucks it away while walking on and murmuring to himself. "Guess everyone already knows the time and location..."

~*~

The residential side-streets on the island of Key West are peaceful and absent of tourists in the late morning hour. Jon strolls carelessly along, delighting in the home-grown sights, sounds and smells of his newly assimilated lifestyle. Turning onto Duval Street, the drone of loud motor-scooters, cars and expensive tourist shops overflowing with raucous vacationers fill the crowded avenue.

Island Stepping with Hemingway

Making his way down the street toward the shipyard, Jon veers off and turns into a small nondescript alleyway. Beneath the overhanging shade of a deep-rooted banyan tree, an aged sign with hand-painted lettering can be made out: *Conch Republic Tavern*. Jon moves through the vacant beer garden of random oddball chairs, café tables and scuff-worn benches before entering the tavern.

The interior of the renowned drinking establishment is furnished and decked out like an Old English seafarer tavern. It has timeworn mariner stylishness, with dark wood panel walls and aged brass fittings in need of a deckhand's polish. Jon steps past the stout entry doors and looks to a decorative plaque fastened to a sawed-off portion of reclaimed ship mast. The fancy lettered inscription reads:

This watering hole has gone by many monikers.
It was a house of ill-repute and a speakeasy during Prohibition,
served as a regular stop for Ernest Hemingway,
and was renamed for 'The Conch Republic' on April 23, 1982
following the succession of the Florida Keys from
The United States of America.

Jon lets his eyes adjust to the low, amber glow of the vintage oil lanterns now converted to electric and gazes over at a pair of bearded fishermen with pints of ale in the corner. He steps into the mostly unpopulated watering hole and lets the heavy door swing closed behind. Jon studies the tavern as he walks over to the carved mahogany bar across the room.

Alone at the bar, Jon throws a leg over a stool and settles in to wait for a reunion with his friend, Scott Fulton. Enjoying the peaceful silence in contrast to the street outside, Jon puts his elbow to the heavily lacquered bar-top and a foot to the lower brass rail. A door opens at the far end of the tavern, and he takes notice as a beautiful, long-haired lady with a bar towel tucked at her waist saunters toward him.

A simply eye-catching female, just over the hump of her middle years, Angie Storm is the owner and operator of the Conch Republic Tavern. She is comfortably known in town as a vocal supporter and activist of local environmental causes and happenings. She seems to manage her business interests and affairs with a healthy blend of beauty and brains. The spindle legs of the bar stool creak on the plank floor as Jon adjusts himself more comfortably on the seat.

Angie stops in front of him and offers a friendly nod. "Hello, what can I be gettin' for ya, fella?" Jon peers down at his overpriced wristwatch in the low lamplight of the tavern. He gazes around the mostly empty barroom and self-consciously replies, "Is it business hours yet?"

"Depends on what sort of thing you're interested in." Angie grins at Jon seductively and hikes a foot up on a box of empty bottles behind the bar. "If you're hungry, we don't serve lunch until just before noon since everyone sleeps late."

"Is it too early for a beer?"

Continuing her charming manner, Angie opens her arms and gestures to the lineup of beer taps behind her. "We're open. Depends on when you got up to start your day… It's never too early for a drink."

Scanning the various logos, Jon points to a bright-colored tapper at the end. "How about that… Sunset Ale?"

The warm sense of infatuation comes over Jon as he watches the attractive saloonkeeper flip a length of hair away from her face, spin a bar glass on her open palm and draw the pint of beer. Her bright, sparkling eyes peer over her rounded shoulder giving a sultry expression which makes Jon's heart pound in his chest. She shoots him a nifty wink as she speaks "So, you're on vacation? Without looking at your expensive timepiece, how long are you here for?"

"Probably a few beers."

V

The female saloonkeeper behind the bar grins and laughs as she turns back to the pour. "How long are you in the Keys?"

"Oh, a while I guess… I'm staying."

She tops off the careful pour. The beer foam drips from the tapper and sits perfectly crowned over the rim of the shiny pint glass. "Where ya from?"

"Southern California."

Angie gives him a sly look. "Oh, you're one of *those*?" Jon acts offended but understands her obvious implication. "Whatever do you mean by 'one of those'?" She snorts and flips a *Conch Republic Tavern* coaster onto the polished bar top before setting the presentation-worthy pint of ale before Jon. "Most types that migrate here from up there buy a charming old house or two, live like a local a few months until the weather gets sticky or a hurricane scares 'em, then move back, bulldoze the house and build rental condos."

Jon takes a short sip from the beer glass in front of him and smiles innocently. "I'm renting... sort of."

Angie hikes a leg up on the box behind the bar again, and leans on her raised knee. "Sorry, I didn't mean to rant. Who you renting from?" Jon seems somewhat surprised at the straightforward questioning from the woman behind the bar. "Do you know everyone on the island?" She offers a shrug and her charming grin lingers. "Everyone worth knowing...?"

Jon gazes around the tavern and takes in the home-grown charm and local history of the island watering hole as he responds. "Through mutual friends, I was hooked up with this interesting gal who said I could stay and do my work as long as I needed. I think she's from France or something."

Angie raises both eyebrows and seems especially interested. "Did you meet with her personally?"

"We exchanged emails."

"Does her name happen to be Jeaneé Reneé?"

"Yes, I think that's how you say it."

Angie nods thoughtful and appears very impressed. "She's quite the intriguing character and owns a lot of coral in these islands. Which property you at?"

"Just off Fleming Street."

Surprised, the attractive bar owner crinkles her brow. "You must really be something kinda special, living in the carriage house apartment."

"You know of it?"

Angie drops her foot to the floor and leans forward on the bar in a perceptive manner. "It's the nature of this type of business. I know most everyone on the island that stays long. If you stick around more than two weeks, I'll probably know quite a bit about you, too." She extends her hand to shake. "Pleased to meet you. Angie Storm, owner-operator of the

Island Stepping with Hemingway

Conch Republic Tavern." Jon takes her slender hand and receives a firm handshake. "Jon Springer, unemployed."

"What sort of work did you do before to make an honest living, Jon Springer?"

"I wrote."

Angie winks. "I said honest living."

"Yep, I'm a writer."

Angie beams a wide, amused grin and nods to the painted portrait of Ernest Hemingway hanging over the bar. "You a Hemingway-type who writes early and then drinks, fishes, or fights the day away, or the kind who just drinks to inspire the creative impulses?" Wide-eyed, Jon takes another sip of his beer and looks up at Angie. "If I need any in-depth character bios for my next stories, I'll know where to come." He sets the pint glass of beer down, rotating it on the coaster. "I'm meeting an old friend here."

Angie paces behind the bar, inspecting the cocktail garnish supplies. "We get quite a few writer-types down here. Maybe it's the island lifestyle, the warm weather or the romantic setting. Anyway, it doesn't last long before they're tail-tucked, heading for the mainland." She takes a folded drink umbrella and puts it between her teeth like a toothpick. "Used to be, all the important literary figures spent time down in the Florida Keys, fishing, writing and hiding away from the rest of the world."

She opens the tiny umbrella and spins it like a top. "Scott Fulton, the world traveling novelist and playwright... He's a regular down here during most of the bigger festivals."

Jon chokes a cough and nearly spits out his swallow of beer. "That's who I'm here to meet."

The tavern owner stops what she's doing, peers up at Jon on the stool across the bar from her and studies him a moment before smiling. "He's done some really great stuff.

I'm not sure if it should all be in the fiction section, though."
Angie seems to read Jon a little closer as she continues... "You
must be quite the wild card or near celebrity to be friends with
Scott Fulton."

"We were roommates once, back in Chicago."

Angie nods her head, viewing Jon in a different light.
"He always has crazy new stories whenever he comes in here.
Have I read anything of yours?"

Jon takes a swig of beer and turns towards the bright
light surrounding the entry door. "Probably not."

Angie follows his gaze toward the entrance and leans
forward on the bar with the tiny umbrella in hand. "Scott and
that other fella, Springs, are two of my favorites."

Pleasantly surprised, Jon swivels around and looks to
Angie. "I've read some from each of them."

"If you're looking to find some good entertaining stuff,
you're in the right place and definitely hanging with the right
sort of people." Angie puts her elbows to the bar top and
heaves her chest up. "They say a writer is like a magic hat."

The bottom of the beer glass sticks to the cardboard
coaster and Jon rotates them both trying not to notice her fine
bosom. He gazes up into her eyes and replies, "How's that?"

With a clever wink, Angie beams at him humorously.
"You have to put something in before you can get anything
out." She raps her knuckles on the wooden bar-top and
saunters away. "Give a holler when Scott finally comes in."
She looks over her shoulder and laughs. "That is, if he doesn't
have a forward entourage to announce his grandiose arrival."
Jon dutifully observes her eye-catching, feminine swagger as
she moves away and he can only muster up an insipid smile
She nudges her rounded hip against the swinging door to the
back supply room and jabs a pointed finger in his direction.

"Go ahead and grab yourself another beer when you need it."
Jon lifts his glass in a saluting answer and watches her exit.

Sitting alone, Jon stares across the bar at the various beer tappers. The two men in the corner drink silently, and the rest of the empty room waits for the afternoon lunch crowd. He gives a shrug, glances to the front entryway and takes another sip of from his cold, sweated pint of beer.

~*~

A plainclothes policeman and a man in maritime uniform stand in front of the U.S. Coast Guard headquarters. In the harbor background, Scott Fulton's sailboat is being towed into the shipyard by a patrol boat. The single tall mast sits at a canted angle with the white hull half sunk below the waterline and floatation buoys surrounding the vessel.

The uniformed Coast Guard officer witnesses the unusual sight of the nearly-scuttled sailboat while he speaks. "It was pretty well sunk when they came across it and about twenty minutes from the point of no return."

The policeman shakes his head, dubious of the situation with the watercraft. "That's not good. Because of whose boat it is, the press here and from the mainland will have a field day with this thing."

The naval officer shrugs, adjusts the visor on his cap and puts his hands to his hips. "Unless there are drugs or a body found, we can't do anything more." The two stand and quietly observe as the semi-submerged sailboat slowly trails the orange and white coast guard vessel through the marina.

VI

The Conch Republic Tavern is beginning to get the afternoon crowd of lunch tourists and regulars. Jon is still sitting on the stool with his elbows perched at the edge of the bar. He peeks over his shoulder as Angie passes by, and she notices him fidget with his empty beer glass. Perceiving that their mutual friend hasn't arrived yet, she comes over and leans on the bar rail alongside him. "You want some lunch?"

Jon eases off the stool, wriggles the flow of blood back into his legs and feet, then stretches his back. He smiles at Angie and looks around the barroom before shaking his head. "No, I'm going to head back to the apartment."

Angie takes his empty beer glass and sets it behind the bar in the sink. "Alright, I'll be sure to point him in the right direction when he finally stumbles in." Her hand touches on his shoulder and a tingle of sensual chemistry charges through his slightly-buzzed being.

Reaching into his pocket, Jon pulls out his wallet and flips it open to pay for his drinks. With a warm smile, Angie puts her hand over his and pushes the folded money away. "Don't worry about it. I'll put this first round on Fulton's tab." She moves down the bar to serve some recent arrivals and casts a waving gesture. "Welcome to the island, Jon Springer."

~*~

The warm heat of midday becomes heavy in the air as the hustling bustle of street commerce happens everywhere. An independent–minded group of chickens scamper across the roadway as Jon walks down the street to his new domicile. He eyes a *Key West Police* vehicle parked across the way from the old house and eyes the slim light bar along the rooftop. Hesitating a moment, Jon looks over the officially painted municipal Jeep then passes through the decorative yard gate, entering the surrounding gardens.

Ascending the spiraled stairway to the carriage house, Jon opens the screen door to the apartment and is received by an unsolicited visitor inside. A uniformed police officer is lounging at ease, leaning on the table next to Jon's computer. The sensation of uneasiness sweeps over Jon as he looks around the invaded apartment for some sort of disturbance. The policeman notices Jon enter the premises, stands upright and addresses him. "Jonathan Tyler Springer?"

Jon looks tentatively at the law officer and then examines the apartment for his friend and former roommate. The presence of a local police officer at his new residence has the elaborate makings of one of Scott Fulton's famous pranks. "Is he here somewhere? Is this a joke, or are you gonna do a funny dance?"

The policeman follows Jon's gaze around the empty room. "Sir, this is not a joke ... and I won't be doing a dance."

Island Stepping with Hemingway

Not feeling at ease with this awkward invasion and unsure of his particular rights, Jon stares at the policeman and tilts his head questioningly. "Did someone invite you in?"

Another person in street clothes comes from the back bedroom. Dressed in casual island attire with a holstered sidearm perched on his trouser hip, he looks to Jon and clears his throat. "The front door was open."

Jon stares at the intruder as the plainclothes officer pulls credentials from his pocket and flips it open to display a detective badge with official looking identification. Uncomfortable with the violation of space, Jon looks to the other officer in uniform and then behind to the open door. "The door was unlocked, not open. There is a difference."

"Detective Peter Lyle, Key West Police Department." The officer tucks away his identification and gruffly adds, "We can step outside to talk if you prefer."

"Do you welcome everyone to the island this way?"

The policeman by the table moves to the doorway, and Detective Lyle gestures for Jon to take a spot on the sofa. "Why don't you have a seat, Mister Springer? We have a few simple questions for you."

Jon steps further into the apartment, looking at his few personal belongings in the room which seem to be intact. "Detective, I might have more than a few questions for you."

The detective motions for Jon to sit and finally asks, "Do you know a Scott Fulton?"

Jon looks to Detective Lyle and tries to figure him out. "Is he in some sort of trouble?"

The detective waits for Jon to seat himself on the sofa and continues. "His sailing vessel was brought in by the Coast Guard this morning from about ten miles off shore." He stares indifferently at Jon. "Do you know anything about that?"

"He need bail money?"

The detective shakes his head as he studies the room. "Mister Fulton wasn't on the boat."

Jon eyes the inquisitive detective again to be sure this isn't another one of Fulton's elaborate shenanigans. The casually-dressed investigator in the tropical shirt could be an imposter, but the uniformed policeman at the doorway seemed legit. Jon quickly considers the state of affairs and decides to go along with the scenario. "So, where is he then, Mister Detective?"

Detective Lyle crosses his stocky arms across his chest and gazes out the front window. "From the transmission of the satellite phone, we figure he was on course for Key West. The Coast Guard towed in an abandoned, half-sunk sailboat. Nobody was on-board and you were the last calls he made."

Starting to realize this might possibly not be in jest, Jon looks at the police detective. "I talked to him earlier this morning. We were supposed to meet for lunch."

Detective Lyle nods and glances over toward the policeman at the door to exchange an unconvinced look. "Where were you to meet?"

"The Conch Republic Tavern."

"You waited for him there?"

"Yes, but obviously he didn't show."

The island detective nods and grumbles aloud. "Anyone see you there?"

"I talked with the owner awhile."

"What did you talk about on the second phone call?"

"I only spoke with him once."

The detective takes out a notepad, writes something down, then looks up and scans his eye around the apartment. "Did he mention any type of problem during your phone conversation or about having to ditch the boat?"

"No."

Island Stepping with Hemingway

After further scrutiny of the main living area, Lyle's stern gaze returns to Jon. "How long have you been here?"

"In this apartment or the island?"

"Both."

Considering his still to be unpacked suitcase across the room, Jon shrugs a reply, "About a week in the Florida Keys and a day or so here in this place."

"How long is your planned stay?"

"A bit longer."

The detective grimaces and turns to the front door. "They have Fulton's boat dry-docked down at the shipyard. The Coast Guard is currently searching for a body, any illegal contraband or anything that might be considered suspicious."

Jon sits the sofa and looks from one officer to the other. "A half-sunk abandoned sailboat isn't suspicious enough?"

The detective seems not to hear the comment and continues. "We'll keep in touch. Be sure to let me know when you plan on leaving the island."

"Am I a suspect or something?"

Detective Lyle moves next to the police officer at the apartment entryway and glances back at Jon on the sofa. "Let's just say, you're a person we have a special interest in."

Jon remains seated and watches the detective push open the screen door. "That's it, only a few questions and no answers? Is that the normal thing down here?"

Detective Lyle holds the door and glares back at Jon. "Hey fella, I've seen stranger things."

"Isn't it your job to find out what happened?"

The irritated detective ushers the policeman outside, hesitates at the doorway a moment and then steps back inside. "Look... I take it you're here on vacation or special holiday. We don't know about your past relationship to Fulton." Detective Lyle leaves his hand on the screen door frame to hold it open. "To tell you the truth, I could care less what's happened to him. I'll do my job and you can do whatever you came down here for." The wood-framed screen door creaks on the spring hinges as the detective steps to the outside again. "Right now, unless you can tell us anything more, that's all there is I can tell you at this time." Detective Lyle pulls a calling card from his shirt pocket and tosses it to the table. "We'll let you know if we find a body. Be sure to call me if you hear from him."

The old screened door slams shut with a loud bang as the police officers make their exit down the spiral stairway. Left alone, Jon sits on the sofa to mull over the bizarre circumstances. He glances over at the old-fashioned rotary telephone that was so active a few hours earlier and then across the room to his closed laptop computer. Standing, he moves to the apartment's front panel of louver-shuttered windows and peers out.

Jon watches the detective and uniformed officer exit through the front yard gate and climb into the police vehicle. A long, quiet moment passes before the vehicle finally pulls forward and rolls down the street. With a creaking-slam of the screen door, Jon steps outside and moves down the winding set of stairs to the garden below.

VII

The interior of the Conch Republic Tavern is filled with a combination of tourists and professional sport fisherman. Jon maneuvers his way through the tables and chairs, bellies up to the bar and gestures to Angie, who is working at the far end. She recognizes him, serves a drink and smiles warmly. Approaching Jon's end of the bar, she searches the crowd behind him for Fulton. "Did ya find him?"

Jon shakes his head dejected and leans over the bar. "No, and neither did the police."

Angie looks at Jon strangely. "You called the police?"

"They were at the garage apartment when I got there. Someone named Detective Lyle and another one. He said the Coast Guard pulled Fulton's sailboat in from a few miles offshore this morning, nearly sunk." The existence of the milling crowd seems to fade as Angie directs her whole attention to Jon and replies, "He wasn't on it?"

Jon tilts his head sadly and gazes across the bar at her. The confused feeling of trauma from the unusual event is just starting to sink in for him. "This is unbelievable. I don't know who I can talk to or what I can do to help try and find him."

She reaches out, putting her hand over his on the bar. "We'll find him." Angie grips his fingers, gives them a compassionate squeeze, and Jon can sense her warm kindness. "Let me talk to someone I know. Stay here a minute."

Angie gives Jon's hand a reaffirming pat and moves down the bar to an elderly guy in a long-billed fishing cap. From the looks of his shabby work-attire and permanently grease-stained hands, he looks to be some sort of mechanic. The old codger hunches over the bar, listening attentively to Angie, and then wipes his thick hand over his face. He looks unhappily at the sweating bottle of beer before him then takes a long, thirst-quenching gulp before slipping from his stool.

The two approach from both sides of the crowded bar. Jon eyes the elderly character curiously, as Angie leans closer to introduce them to each other. "Jon, this is Ace. He is chief mechanic and voice of reason over at Key West Air Charters."

Jon extends his hand to shake and winces from the strong, vice-like grip of the mechanic's oversized, work-stained mitt. "Jon Springer... Pleased to meet you."

The mechanic gives a friendly nod followed by what seems to be a twinkle in his eye. "Ace Milton. Angie tells me you be needin' some kinda help."

Jon glances to Angie, who offers a heartening smile. He turns to the old mechanic. "I'm not sure what anyone can do."

The helpful tavern owner reaches over and rests her hand on Ace's broad shoulder. "Take him over to the hanger." She goes over to a payphone on the wall at the end of the bar. "I'll call Rollie and tell him to get to work on the coast guard."

Island Stepping with Hemingway

Ace gestures Jon toward the entryway and ambles toward it. "You heard the lady. Let's git."

Jon doesn't quite seem to know how to take the odd situation and trustingly follows Ace to the door. He glimpses back at Angie, as she lifts the handset from the wall mounted phone and puts it to her ear. "Thanks for your help, Angie."

She gives a wave before she begins to press in the telephone number. "Scott Fulton is a friend. The guys will take care of you." Turning to follow the old mechanic, Jon walks out the tavern doorway into the bright midday sunlight.

~*~

An old, rusted-over antique pickup truck drives past the Key West International Airport and crosses the bridge to Stock Island to the east of Key West. The truck pulls off highway A1A and pulls up to a neglected and time-worn airplane hangar. A decrepit chain link fence surrounds a large cement pad with a ramp leading down to the water.

Parked out in front of the dome-shaped metal structure, a high-winged Grumman seaplane sits positioned, ready to venture out into the expanse of open sea. Just inside the tall, double hung doors; another World War II era flying boat sits in various stages of deterioration while awaiting restoration. The weather-faded signage at the peak of the dome reads:

Key West Air Charters – adventure, danger, romance

Ace stops the old pickup truck in front of the arched aviation building and looks over at his uncertain passenger. Jon peers out the partially rolled-down truck window at the old, painted letters over the track for the wide, hangar doors. "Is that the company motto?"

Ace shrugs innocent. "Two out of three ain't bad."

Jon responds, "Depends which two."

The aged features of the old mechanic pull back to a wider grin as he swings open his door with a loud creak. "Depends on the day."

Appearing from the ramshackle aviation hangar, dressed in rumpled khaki pants and a button down shirt, Rolland 'Rollie' McKinny appears with a welcoming smile along with a busted, swollen lip and slightly blackened eye. Despite his appearance, he has an alluring air of confidence about him and happy-go-lucky demeanor. The bushy-haired, unkempt seaplane pilot stops just outside the hanger doors and calls over to the recently arrived duo at the old truck. "Hey there, Ace..."

Ace swings the driver's door shut with a creaking bang and moves past the curved wheel-well of the truck's fender. He looks to the seaplane pilot's recent shiner and grimaces. "You lose any bouts recently?" Aside to Jon he mutters, "Rollie likes to think of himself as a pugilist of sorts."

Rollie smiles through his busted lip and puts up his dukes in a fighter's pose. He winks at Jon and makes an imaginary jab and uppercut. "You should see the other guy. He's still in the hospital."

Ace moves beside Jon and leans over to lowly whisper, "Probably because he works there."

The seaplane pilot throws a few more shadow boxing jabs and then swipes back the mussed hair from his forehead. "Sandy called a minute ago and said she'd be in later today." Rollie steps forward and looks up to the seaplane on the pad. "Could you take a minute to look at the left engine? It seems to be running a little rich." Ace turns his attention to the high-winged amphibious seaplane parked above the water ramp. He stares at the tell-tale markings of blackened exhaust trailing behind the radial engine.

Island Stepping with Hemingway

The mental gears of the mechanic's gaze seem to grind steadily and expressively display themselves on the lines of his concentrated features. Ace seems to forget all about Jon as he scratches his chest through his shirt. "Yeah, somethin' was soundin' different when you took 'er out yesterday mornin'. I'll give that engine a look-over and adjust the fuel mixture."

Rollie seems appreciative as Ace goes to a wheeled tool cart near the hangar door and lifts the lid. The seaplane pilot turns back to the pickup truck and puts his attention on Jon. "You the friend of Fulton's?"

"Jon Springer."

He reaches out and gives Jon a warm handshake. "Rollie McKinny. Angie called from the Conch a bit ago and said you were coming." The seaplane pilot claps Jon along the shoulder with his free hand then gestures toward the junk-cluttered interior of the domed aviation hangar. "Come on into the office, and we'll see what we can come up with."

VIII

Just inside the large, spread open hangar doors, Jon follows Rollie past the vintage flying boat restoration project and into a cluttered office space. The seaplane pilot moves around behind a double-wide partner desk, piled high with stacks of papers, aviation books and seemingly random engine parts. Rollie turns to an architect's storage bin of drawers and cubbyholes filled with rolled tubes and folded ocean charts. He speaks over his shoulder, across the systematized disarray. "I had a chat with the coast guard dispatcher just before you drove up. They were reluctant at first, but finally gave me the quadrants where they found Fulton's boat." The seaplane pilot opens and closes a few of the shallow drawers and then pokes through the stack of tubes. "About had them sweet-talked for more info when they got another call and clammed up on me." Rollie draws out a nautical chart from the bin and makes space to spread it out across the clutter on the desk.

Jon peers at the unfamiliar markings for depth and ocean current on the island map. "Can we do anything the police force isn't already doing?"

Rollie glimpses up at Jon from across the desk and smirks. "Pretty much anything we do is more."

"Why is that?"

The seaplane pilot turns his attention back to the map, rolls it aside and unfolds another layout of the Florida Keys. He reaches underneath the displayed grid of the islands, rattles the bell on the desk phone and slides out a pen and notepad of paper with a range of coordinates scribbled on it. Rollie studies the list of numbers against their position on the chart to the west of the main islands and glances briefly at Jon. "You know that Scott often frequented down here?"

Jon nods assenting and observes from across the desk. "Yeah... He would mention it sometimes when we visited."

The seaplane pilot holds the pad of paper with the estimated positioning given by the coast guard and looks up at Jon with a mischievous glimmer in his eyes. Rollie stifles a chuckle, grins widely and gazes back down at the ocean map. "He would have stayed longer ..." Rollie studies the latitude lines and determines the particular location on the chart. "Except every time he came down here, he ended up bucking the fuzz and in lockup before the end of festival."

"A Detective Lyle by any chance?"

Rollie looks up at Jon and the grin sags from his face. "Yeah. You know him?"

With a nod, Jon looks to the map. "He's the one who told me Scott was missing."

"It figures."

Jon continues to observe the pilot plotting on the map. "Scott does get wild sometimes." Rollie traces his finger along the longitudinal lines and chuckles. "Let's just say that the

Island Stepping with Hemingway

Key West Police Department isn't at the top of his fan roster."
Tapping his finger on the map, Rollie indicates the location.
"One more high-profile troublemaker off the dock watch-list
is no sweat for them."

Starting to realize that his celebrated author friend,
Scott Fulton, wasn't as universally loved in the islands as he
had previously imagined, Jon returns his attention to the
nautical chart. "Is that where they picked up his sailboat?"

Rollie circles his finger on a general area west of the
islands. "Dropping down from New Orleans, the currents run
this way across here. It's near the Quicksands and that's
where we'll start looking."

Jon nods, pretending to understand and then looks up,
questioningly, from the ocean chart to the water-flying pilot.
"What's the Quicksands?"

Rollie prudently folds the nautical chart of the location
and grabs a canvas flight bag from the top of the file cabinet.
"That's an area to the west of the Marquesas Islands kinda like
an underwater desert. If you hit the Gulf Stream nearby,
you're on an express current to Ireland." He opens the flight
duffle on the desk and tucks in the map. From the desk chair,
he grabs a sweater and a palm-patterned set of swim trunks.

Jon looks at the shorts as they are stuffed in the canvas
tote and questions Rollie. "What are the swim trunks for?"

Rollie crinkles his forehead playfully. "Swimming?"

"You mean, like if we crash?"

The seaplane pilot takes a silent moment to consider
the contents of the flight bag and looks up to Jon confused.
"No... Like if we put down on the water and want to go for a
midday swim." He grins at Jon with a funny sort of regard.
"Did you say *crash*? Who do you think you're flying with?"

Jon shrugs innocently. "This is all pretty new to me."

"What sort of work do you do?"

The paperback novelist hesitates answering the question, then finally responds. "I'm a writer."

Rollie smiles with interest. "You write books?"

"Yeah, mostly books."

"Like Scott?"

"Sort of."

"Anything I've read?"

Not wanting to flaunt his extensive adventure-writing credentials at this particular meeting, Jon scans the clutter of paperwork and books on the desk. He spots a tattered copy of his early novella – *Pilgrimage of the Jungle by J.T. Springs* – sitting atop assorted water-flying magazines.

"Probably not."

Rollie continues tossing items into his open flight bag. "Well, take some notes and you might have something exciting to write about." He opens a wood slide drawer on the desk, peers inside and then up at Jon. "You have a gun?"

Not aware of his jaw perceptibly sagging, Jon witnesses Rollie take a revolver out from the desk with a box of ammunition. As the seaplane pilot begins to load the handgun, Jon attempts not to stammer... "I think I can understand bringing along the swim trunks, but what do we need a gun for?"

Rollie finishes inserting cartridges into the revolving cylinder of the pistol and turns to Jon with a surprised look. "What do you think exactly has happened to Scott Fulton?"

Clueless, Jon shrugs. "I'm not sure..."

The seaplane pilot cradles the loaded handgun in his open palm and aligns the one remaining empty chamber under the hammer as he lowers it. "A sailboat does not just find itself abandoned and half-sunk in clear blue waters in the gulf for no reason."

Island Stepping with Hemingway

Jon takes a quick second to assess the cluttered office, airplane hangar and abnormal circumstances he seems to have found himself in. "How exactly *does* it happen?"

Rollie peers past Jon's shoulder to the doorway, cautious-like, as if someone could be listening. "When Angie phoned me today, she said that the Key West police were waiting for you this afternoon with questions."

Jon is hesitant but answers, "Yes, that Detective Lyle and another one."

"Why did they go straight to you?"

After thinking a moment, Jon tentatively responds. "Fulton's satellite phone was on the boat with a call history showing I was the last one he talked with."

"They traced the phone number?"

"I guess so."

"Was there a ransom note?"

Jon lifts up his hands and holds both palms forward, shaking his head incredulously at the kidnapping suggestion. "You actually think Fulton was hijacked?"

Rollie tilts his chin and sets the revolver on the desk alongside the flight duffle. The seaplane pilot unexpectedly grabs another auto handgun from the desk drawer and checks the ammo load in the clip. "He's well known for carrying lots of cash when he travels."

A bit confused and definitely out of his usual element, Jon attempts to understand the inconceivable information. "Who would want to do something like that?"

"Pirates."

Jon seems aghast. "Like sword and eye-patch pirates?"

A smirk crosses over Rollie's features as he gazes up at Jon. "No... Like machine guns and high-speed yacht pirates."

"You're kidding?"

The seaplane pilot smacks the loaded ammunition clip into the butt of the handle on the automatic pistol and snorts, "The Caribbean has a rich history of it and is full of 'em." Rollie puts the loaded auto pistol inside the canvas duffle. "Who do ya think does the smuggling down in these parts?"

Jon glances to the six-shot revolver next to the flight bag, as the desperado seaplane pilot continues with his possible scenario. "The mainland newspapers don't really talk about the pirates much unless there is a big drug bust or it's a slow day in Washington... or Hollywood." Rollie grabs a box of crackers from the top of the fridge and tucks them in the duffle as well. After zipping the bag closed, Rollie slides the gun across the desk to Jon. "You know how to use that thing?"

Jon stares at the revolver on the desktop and nods meekly as Rollie moves alongside, patting him on the arm. "Alright, let's go get to hunting. It could get chilly up there." The seaplane pilot pulls an extra jacket from the back of a chair and puts it into Jon's arms as he grabs up the flight bag. He offers the noticeably stunned writer a reassuring grin and steps out of the office. "Shake a leg, Springer!"

Jon's dazed stare lingers over the loaded revolver then travels again to his dog-eared, paperback adventure story mixed with the pile of desk clutter. As if moving in a daydream, he lifts the pistol and tucks it in the jacket pocket. He holds the bundled firearm and quietly murmurs aloud, "What the hell did I get myself into?"

IX

Outside the double hangar doors of Key West Air Charters, Jon watches as Ace shuffles past a step ladder, pushing the upright tool chest clear of the troublesome radial engine. Through the small forward window on the flying boat, Jon can see the pilot already inside the cockpit of the seaplane. Watching Rollie getting situated in the captain's chair behind the controls gives Jon a queasy dose of reality.

Holding the wrapped bundle of jacket and handgun, Jon walks past the torpedo-shaped pontoon float that hangs down a few feet from the wing tip. He approaches the hatch door at the rear tail-section as the propellers begin to rotate and the radial engines rumble, belching out heavy exhaust. Ace stands near the short ladder leading to the open hatch and hands Jon a tool bag as he ascends.

The mechanic grins at Jon and raises his voice to holler above the noisy sound of the warming airplane engines.

"Couldn't find anything wonky with that old engine without tearing it all apart. It should be serviceable for today mostly."

At the top of the ladder, Jon yells back questioningly. "For today?"

Ace grins broader and pats Jon along the pants leg. "It'll be fine. That's why you got two."

Jon climbs inside the seaplane's cargo hold, sets the bag of tools aside and turns back to Ace as the old timer pulls the laddered stairway away. The sharp-eyed mechanic sees the gun barrel poking out from the bundled jacket in Jon's arms and the smile instantly fades from his features. Ace calls out to Jon, just over the engine noise, "Don't ever think to doubt 'em. Them sort of folks mean business."

Jon nods and holds to the inner framework of the flying boat hatch as Ace turns away. The gust created from the whirling propellers blows past, as he looks out to the quaint Air Charter headquarters neighboring the industrial vicinity.

Rollie calls back from the cockpit, "All set back there?"

Reluctant, Jon peers forward, then swings the seaplane's rear access door closed and secures the latch. He makes his way through the cargo hold and double row of seats to the forward section of the seaplane. He slides into the copilot chair and tucks the gun wrapped jacket between his feet, under the seat. Rollie glances over at him, flashes a confident smile and then gives a thumbs-up signal to Ace outside the window. "Ready for this?"

"Yeah, I guess... Ready as I'll ever be."

With one hand on the yoke and his feet on the brakes, the seaplane pilot reaches overhead and eases both engine throttles forward in sync. The whirling propellers on the revving engines spin and become almost transparent, like disks of glass. The dual overhead radials roar as the props seem to fade away then almost appear to spin backward.

Island Stepping with Hemingway

From the wide hangar doorway, Ace watches as the Grumman seaplane's engines roar and the extended wheels, mid frame from the boat hull, slowly creak and ease ahead. The seaplane rolls forward and descends down the cement ramp into the shallow, clear blue waters encircling the island. A spray of mist blows back behind the whirling propellers as the high-winged amphibian travels out to the watery depths. In deeper water, the body of the seaplane settles in to the windows and wing floats and starts to bobble afloat, as the landing wheels slowly retract into the hull.

The twin radials belch exhaust, roaring to full throttle. Low in the water, the seaplane races across the aqua-blue surface, leaving a wake of white misty spray and a cascading wave of ocean peeling back from its stepped hull. The flying boat lifts and separates from the water's surface, taps down slightly with a small splash and then leaps into the air again. Now airborne, the boat-shaped body and high mounted wings bank to the horizon of the western sky.

~*~

In flight, the vibrating hum of the synchronized radial engines becomes a steady drone that tickles the inner-ear. Seated on the right chair, Jon stares out the copilot window at the endless stretch of ocean water below. After a long while, his eyes begin to drift and tire from the unending pattern of rolling waves, marine shoals and continuous blue seascapes. He shifts in his seat and turns to Rollie, who has the marine chart spread over his lap. "What are we looking for exactly?"

The seaplane pilot looks up from the nautical map, rechecks his flight instruments and peers out the window. "We're going to do a grid pattern over the area where the coast guard found the boat and spot for anything unusual."

"This whole situation is unusual for me."

Rollie peers over his left shoulder to the water below and shifts the partially folded ocean map aside from his lap. He puts on a playful grin as he adjusts the overhead throttles. "It's just another average day at the office for me. Welcome to life in the islands!" The seaplane pilot pushes the yoke forward and the airplane dips to a dive at the water's surface. In the copilot chair, Jon puts his hands forward attempting to hold onto the framework and brace himself in the seat.

Outside, the dual engines whine as they careen toward the aquatic surface, easing up just shy of the rolling waves. The Grumman flying boat wings low over gentle seas in almost cloudless skies. On the vast panorama of ocean, nothing appears unusual to the naked eye for miles around. The seaplane races only a few feet above the water's surface with schools of fish, sea turtles and other marine wildlife discernable in the ocean depths below.

Banking near the perimeter of the planned grid, the seaplane engines fade and roar again as they come around. Jon presses his face to the cold surface of the side window and tries to keep his stomach from rising into his dry throat. Peering outside, he jabs his finger to the window where he notices an object floating in the water. "I see something!"

Rollie glances at his eager passenger, as he brings the low-flying seaplane around. He sits high in the seat and gazes over the instrument panel as he calls out, "What do you see?"

"I don't know... Might be some sort of buoy."

The seaplane pilot pulls up the forward nose of the aircraft and makes another hard turn to circle back again. With his hand manipulating the dual overhead throttles, Rollie speaks loudly to Jon to compete with the noise of the engines outside. "Probably just a bit of ocean trash, but we'll check it out." The seaplane banks and dives at the water, almost skimming the surface with its curved belly.

Island Stepping with Hemingway

In the copilot seat, Jon tightens his lap belt and swallows hard to keep down the contents of his stomach, as the seaplane dips and dives along the cresting tips of waves. Jon squints apprehensively toward Rollie while the searching pilot sits upright, peering out the forward and side windows. "Is it legal to fly this low?"

Rollie keeps his attention focused on flying as he smiles, self-assured. He keeps his left hand gripped on the steering yoke as the other hand reaches overhead, spreading deft fingers between the pairing of the dual engine throttles. "In a seaplane it is... at least over unregulated open water." The pilot glances over at his passenger with a guilty grimace. "When I fly near Cuba or their military airspace, I like to call 'em *long* approaches." As the seaplane banks slightly, Rollie reaches alongside his seat and passes Jon a set of binoculars. He points over the instrument panel at the wide expanse of ocean below. "Is that what you saw?"

Jon puts the distance-glasses to his face and tries to locate the intended object. After adjusting focus, he finally zeros in and makes out a military gray item drifting afloat. "Yeah, that's it... Looks to be a boat seat cushion maybe."

Rollie nods and pulls back the throttles as he eases the airplane's yoke forward. "I'm going to put 'er down."

The seaplane touches down on the water's surface, jolting the binoculars from Jon's face. The queasy passenger pushes back in the seat as the descending seaplane settles on the curved step-hulled belly. Heavy sprays of water splash past the window, and the occasional ocean chop mists through spinning propellers.

Taxiing the seaplane across the water's surface like a speedboat, Rollie steers the amphibious craft toward the abandoned floating object. The speeding seaplane gently begins to slip and drift sideways as the wing flaps and tail rudder veer the vessel around into a wide-arcing semi-circle. As he eases back both overhead throttles a touch more, the winged watercraft slows and settles lower in the water.

With white knuckles gripped at the edge of his seat frame, Jon glimpses over at Rollie behind the controls. He takes a calming breath, looks out the near window and utters, "Can you pull up next to it?"

The seaplane pilot gooses the starboard engine, turning the plane slightly in the direction of the unidentified object. He reaches down between the seats into his flight bag and tosses the swim trunks onto Jon's lap. "I can get pretty close, but you might need those."

In disbelief, Jon looks down at the tropical-patterned swimsuit and back at Rollie. "You can't get closer than that?"

Rollie works the tail rudder on the floating seaplane to angle straighter into the wind and makes an adjustment to both of the throttles. "This isn't any kind of exact science. Jump back there and see if you can hook it with the anchor line first." Entirely out of his element, Jon stares at Rollie skeptically, and they exchange an uncertain look. The pilot shrugs modestly. "Jokes aside pal, its what's got to be done." Jon takes a moment to collect himself, unbuckles his lap belt and maneuvers his way to the back cargo hold.

Positioned at the rear hatch, Jon unlatches the door and swings it to the interior. He looks out to the undulating surface of dark blue waters just below the opened doorway. As Jon looks toward the cockpit of the aircraft, Rollie peeks around to the cargo cabin and calls out, "I have to swing wide. If it passes under the propeller it could catch a rising swell and tear it up."

A gentle ocean breeze blows in through the opening, as Jon stares outside and nods. "Fine. Get as close as you can." Jon holds the edge of the hatch and leans out to look around

Island Stepping with Hemingway

He spots the floating object several yards away and judges its approximate distance. Pulling his head back inside, he studies the coil of marine rope tied to the anchor and then yells up to Rollie at the controls. "The anchor idea isn't going to work. Can you get any closer to it?"

The seaplane rolls and pitches on the waves, as Rollie looks back from the flight controls with an amused smirk. "You'll just have to sport the swim trunks, buddy. I'll bring us around for another pass."

Jon looks outside at the deep, blue water and yells back toward Rollie in the cockpit. "What about sharks?"

Rollie peers over his shoulder out the side windows and hollers back to the cargo hold, "I don't see any, do you?"

Jon sticks his head out the open hatch and looks down into the watery depths. "Ah, crap…" Back inside, he pulls his shirt off, unlaces his shoes to kick them away and reaches for the swim trunks.

X

The sky is blue and the ocean surface calm, as the midday sun shines bright over the luxury pirate yacht coming to anchor. High amidships, on the bridge of the sleek black vessel, a large, wide panel of dark window glass shimmers and mirrors the surrounding ocean like a looming pair of the ever-watching sunglasses from *Cool Hand Luke*. Mirrored in the reflected glass window pane is a small uninhabited island situated to the starboard bow.

A camo-clad, figure comes from the rear of the yacht with a Glock handgun and survival knife strapped at his side. Jacek, the first mate, is an urban mercenary with a manner hardened from both soldierly combat and life on the high seas. He passes by a compact, twin-engine speedboat suspended at the rear of the ship and nimbly climbs the outer stairway to the upper bulwarks.

Jacek taps out a courtesy knock before entering the ship's bridge and stops short at the overhead-lit entry. Narrowing his eyes, he gazes toward the darker interior of the command center. Captain Longley remains unmoved in his stance, with wide shoulders pulled back and both hands clasped behind him. His features in shadow, the captain looks out through the tinted panes of observation windows. Without turning around to greet him, Longley addresses the first mate. "Is our special guest, Mister Fulton, sociable yet?"

Jacek stands ramrod straight with his feet spread hips-width apart. The first mate's heavy brow and hard-lined features seem to glower in the harsh lighting from above. Clenching his gloved fists before his torso, he responds directly. "He has an affluent friend staying on the island."

The profile of the captain's chin nods slightly, as he continues to stare forward out the dark-tinted windows. Captain Longley, deliberately taking a slow lungful of air, continues to stare forward as his shoulders heave upward. "Does this friend have ample financial resources to complete the ransom for Mister Fulton and to supplant the material and opportunity cost of our lost cargo?"

"From what I got out of him, this author fellow should be able to cover it, easy."

Captain Longley turns his head slightly to reveal a shadowed portion of his profile. "What is his name?"

"J.T. Springs."

A subtle look of acknowledgement registers on the pirate captain's features as he recognizes the well-known adventure author's name. Silhouetted against the windows, Longley silently ponders the state of affairs and finally nods agreeably. He turns his gaze, once again, out the panel of tinted windows and unclasps his hands from behind.

Island Stepping with Hemingway

The pirate captain reflexively touches his palm to his upper right abdomen, and winces noticeably as he draws his fingers away from the recent shooting injury. A slight glance down reveals traces of fresh blood on his crisp uniform shirt. The first mate stands under the harshly-lit entry in dutiful silence until the captain clears his throat to utter his orders. "Deliver the ransom message to the writer-friend in Key West. Be sure to convey that Mister Fulton's life depends on it."

"Yes, Sir." Jacek snaps off a military salute, takes a step backward and spins on his heel before exiting the chamber. The ship rolls slightly on a passing swell and settles again. With the small, uninhabited island and open sea before him, Captain Longley continues to stare out as he speaks aloud to the empty room. "This author personage, Mister Springs, will pay dearly for our mutual comrade's misjudgment at sea."

~*~

The Grumman seaplane cruises boat-like on the surface of the ocean and cuts a wide circling path through the waves. The big radial engines momentarily roar and spray seawater, then cut to a rumbling idle. Inside the seaplane's cargo hold, Jon stands exposed at the open rear hatch, dressed in the swim trunks with the tethered line from the anchor fastened around his midsection. He pushes back from the hatch and looks to Rollie in the cockpit with a worried expression. "What about those spinning propellers?"

The seaplane pilot leans over in his seat and looks back into the rear cargo area to holler. "Be sure to stay behind 'em! Don't want to cut the engines completely or I won't have any sort of directional control. You have about fifty feet of slack on that rope, after that, you're going to get pulled along."

Jon glimpses at the rolling ocean waves outside the open hatch and yells over the engine noise to the cockpit. "You mean I'll be dragged along like human chum?"

"Yeah, something like that. I'll try to do a wide arc and give you a bit more time with that tether line."

Jon tosses the extra length of rope out of the open rear hatch and watches the line uncoil. The floating strands of marine cord slowly drift behind and fade into the choppy wake of the seaplane. Eyes closed and taking a deep breath, Jon puts his toes to the edge of the door hatch and dives out into the rising blue swells.

The cruising seaplane bobs among the uneven waves as the high-winged radial engines rumble at just above an idle. As Jon pops to the surface, the propellers continue to whirl with intermittent wisps of ocean spray churning through them. He looks around a short moment and pushes his wet hair back from his face. With overhand strokes, he starts forward toward the distant, floating object.

The ocean waves carry Jon as he swims with strong, reaching paddles, while the seaplane slowly moves in a wide half-circle, drifting farther away. A slight tugging from the rope around his waist turns Jon around to see the slack of the tether-line riding over the swells. Finally reaching the floating object, Jon grabs ahold of the dark item and turns it over. After a quick inspection, the article appears to be a military surplus-style combat/life vest.

Jon gazes to his boat-plane transport a short distance away and lashes the vest to the tail-end of his safety rope. Seemingly alone in the water, Jon peers down into the aqua depths at the shifting sands and the variety of sea-life below. He begins to pull himself back to the seaplane and gets a dunking face-full of ocean surf as he rolls to the side and hauls himself in, hand over hand, along the tethered lifeline.

Finally beside the slow-cruising amphibious aircraft, Jon pulls himself in through the rear doorway hatch and drops to the floor. Dripping wet and heaving for air like a fresh-caught fish, Jon lays on the metal floor of the seaplane. The seaplane pilot pivots in his seat and peers back. Rollie taps the throttles, gestures a thumb upward and grins wide. "You okay back there...? What have you got?"

Jon rolls over and tosses the limp, wet form of the floatation item toward the cockpit. "An old life vest is all."

Still seated at the controls, Rollie reaches back, grabs up the sopping wet, cloth-covered military vest and inspects it. He turns it over to look for any markings or identification. "Military grade... Wonder what caliber that bullet hole is?"

Jon takes another heaving breath and rises to his feet. He stumbles toward the front of the seaplane and pokes his head in the cockpit to look over Rollie's shoulder to the vest. "Did you say bullet hole?"

The pilot glances behind at the water-glistened figure in the dripping pair of swim trunks. "You're lucky there wasn't the remainder of a body in this when you found it."

Jon stares at the small entry hole of a bullet along the abdomen with the ragged exit point on the vest's backside. Upon closer inspection to the interior, faint stains of blood surround the pass-through locations on the dark wet fabric. An involuntary shiver surges through Jon's body as he replies, "Any thoughts about where it came from?"

Rollie ponders the life vest a moment as the seaplane continues to idly cruise forward in the open ocean waters. "Whoever was wearing this probably survived the injury, or they threw the body overboard separately."

"Why do you say that?"

Rollie snorts teasingly. "Or, there'd be teeth marks."

The seaplane pilot watches Jon seem to go pale, as he stands dripping and staring in disbelief at the bullet hole. Rollie holds up the combat life jacket and offers it to the astounded passenger. "Here, take this in the back with you.

Shut that rear hatch, grab a towel and we'll get out of here." The seaplane pilot returns his attention out the windscreen to the forward horizon and begins his pre-fight checklist.

The seaplane bobs and tilts in the rolling waters, as the rear hatch swings shut and the radial engines belch exhaust while throttling up. Both engines simultaneously roar with the increase of power, but a cloud of heavy dark smoke blows back from the serviced engine behind the spinning propellers. The amphibious plane lunges forward and the stepped-hull is quickly speeding high along the water's surface. After a short takeoff run, the Grumman flying boat smashes through a rising swell and leaps into the air.

XI

At the waterfront headquarters for Key West Air Charters, the Grumman seaplane stands on the cement parking pad outside the hangar. The high, engine-mounted wings stand perched above the ocean ramp, as an attractive female in a skinny bikini top, cut-off shorts and flip-flops holds a length of canvas-weave fire hose. The bursting jet of water washes the ocean salt from the seams of the aircraft's metal skin while the arching spray deflects off in a rainbow of drenching mist.

Inside the aviation hangar, in the small corner office, the engrossed men are positioned around the partner desk. Ace, Rollie and Jon all stare down at the military-style life jacket laid out on a scrap piece of plastic covering the desktop. The mechanic lifts up a corner of the damp vest and studies it for any identifying marks or labels as he speaks. "Well, it's not from L.L. Bean. They usually don't put in armor plating and a custom shoulder holster to conceal small arms."

Ace grunts, "I was to guess, I'd say its Cuban Military."

Jon looks up at Ace and then turns to Rollie, mystified. "You think the Cubans have something to do with this?"

Rollie shrugs as he watches Ace look the vest over. "Cain't ever tell with these things."

Obviously having a hard time grasping the unusual situation, Jon stammers, "What do you mean *these things*?"

The seaplane pilot continues to observe the senior mechanic's inspection, while Ace thoughtfully rubs his chin whiskers and speaks. "When it comes to illegal smugglers here in the islands, almost anything is possible 'n then some." The military looking armored vest is turned over on the desk again and splayed open to reveal the shoulder holster inside. Ace gestures to some tiny inked marking on the lower inside corner of the vest seam. "It's a Russian make alright."

Jon seems the most out of his element in this particular instance, despite his prolific vocation as an adventure writer. His jaw slackens and drops in shock. "Did I hear Russians?"

The seaplane pilot turns to Jon and observes him seeming more ill at ease than when he was a flight passenger. "It's not unusual. Most of Cuba's military was supplied by the Russians after the missile crisis."

Rollie lifts up the damp, outer shell of the life vest and turns it over in his hands. He studies it and then glimpses across the desk to Ace, as they focus on the obvious bullet hole put below the reinforced area protecting the chest cavity. "Ace, who else would be able to get their hands on this make of armored life vest?"

With a scratching sound, Ace deliberately rubs the white whisker stubble along his chin while thinking aloud. "The Cubans don't exactly sell off any of their surplus gear... At least not since the embargo..."

Island Stepping with Hemingway

Jon takes a few steps back and drops uncomfortably on a magazine-cluttered chair. He watches Rollie and Ace carefully inspect the bullet's entry and exit points on the vest. The seaplane pilot puts his smallest finger in the penetrated void to size it up. "Think it's a .45 auto?"

Ace eyes the hole and shrugs uncertain as he turns the vest over to see the dark-stained exit hole. "I dunno, could very well be a .44 Russian?"

There is a soft, interrupting knock outside the office entryway and the glass-paneled door gently swings ajar. Waiting at the threshold in her wet bikini outfit, the eye-catching seaplane detailer pulls her damp hair into a ponytail. Rollie glances up at the girl, lowers the military vest to the desk and grins welcoming. "Hello there, Sandy. Come on in."

She smiles in return and wipes her wet palms on her bare thighs. "Sorry to bother y'all."

"Not a problem." Rollie leans forward on the desktop, and his gaze travels to Jon slunk in the chair near the door. "Have you met Jon Springer here?"

Sandy adjusts her clinging shorts, cut high on slender legs, and rubs her hands together in an attempt to dry them. Jon stands and a stack of airplane magazines slides to the floor at his heels as he extends his hand. "Pleased to meet you."

Sandy shakes Jon's hand and turns to address the seaplane pilot and mechanic "Guys, the water-bird is cleaned-up and tucked-in for the day. Rollie, I was planning to go over the supply orders and verify the schedule for the week." She adjusts her slim bikini top as she watches Jon stoop down to pick up the fallen magazines. She smiles at the usual disorder and looks to Ace at the desk. "If you might need my help with that engine overhaul, I'll be glad to stick around."

The grizzled old mechanic shifts his attention to the attractive, young assistant and adjusts his mindset from

Russian espionage to aircraft maintenance. "Sure, I'll go ove it with you in a bit when I'm done here."

Jon witnesses Sandy's bikini-outfitted departure fron the doorway and then chances to meet Rollie's appreciativ gaze after her. The observant seaplane pilot grimaces guiltily "We hired her because of her training in aircraft mechanics."

Ace shakes his head at them both and grunts hi disapproval. "She's a damn good wrench-monkey, toc Better'n someone else I know who can somehow damag more during a flight than he knows how to fix in a week."

Rollie sits in the reclining desk-chair to get a bette view out the doorway. "That's why I have you around, Ace." Together, Jon and Rollie can't keep from following the aircraf apprentice's sauntering exit out the hangar doors, their head tilting in appreciation of the privileged scenery.

Ace interrupts their obvious gawking with a cough anc straightens his torso. "You should probably see if Carlos is ir town. He might be able to find out where this came from."

Kicked back in the creaking desk chair, Rollie shifts hi distracted attention back to Ace. "Did you happen to see hin this afternoon at the Conch?"

Ace taps grease-stained fingertips on dry puckered lips "Barely had time to enjoy a sip of my beverage before I wai waylaid by Springer here." Resting on his large knuckles, the mechanic leans over the desktop and looks to Jon.

Realizing that most of day has gotten away from him Jon glances at his watch. "Is there anything else can we do?"

Rollie grabs up the military life jacket and tosses i across the room to Jon. He yanks the sheet of plastic from the desktop and wads it up in the corner. "We can meet with Carlos and find out where this vest might have come from."

Jon peers down at the bullet damaged item questioningly. "Who's Carlos?"

XII

The older-model pickup truck with faded paint lettering on the door crosses town, cruising through working-class neighborhoods interspersed with designer vacation rentals. On the passenger side of the sun-bleached bench seat, Jon stares out the rolled-down truck window with a writer's eye. "There is quite the mix of houses on this end of the island."

Rollie glances over at several goats eating grass along a front yard fence and nods, "The island isn't very big, but there are a lot of all types shuffled together here, old and new."

"Seems to make for some interesting characters."

"Yeah, and things seem to be changing every day." Rollie muscles the old truck, lacking any power-steering, around a corner and grunts. "If you enjoy character, wait 'till you get a taste of who we're gonna see next."

"Should we call this Carlos person first?"

The old truck creaks and groans, as some loose items roll and clatter across the pickup bed. His hand gripping the polished 'suicide knob' on the oversized steering wheel, Rollie cranks the tires straight again and shakes his head. "Carlos is kinda funny that way. If someone has an eye out for him and he doesn't want to be seen, you'll never find him."

Jon gazes out the windshield as the truck rolls to a stop at a four way intersection then shifts and rumbles on again. "What does he do for a job on the island?"

"Something related to foreign government and politics. Not tied with much here in the States though. He's tight with some radical Cuban Politicos. He just likes to be in Key West, spending most his time. Figures he won't get shot, I guess." The seaplane pilot turns the pickup truck down an alleyway, hunkers low behind the big steering wheel and murmurs, "That little miscreant..."

Jon turns to Rollie, who crouches in the driver's seat and then looks ahead over the hood of the truck. "Who do you think you are hiding from? Do you see Carlos?"

Rollie straightens up in the truck seat, shifts the engine down a gear and grips both hands firm on the steering wheel. "I'm going to throttle that little imp this time."

The old pickup truck slowly idles forward toward a gangly, juvenile street urchin with yellow-rimmed sunglasses. In his early adolescence, Casey Kettles entertains a group of oblivious tourists with his magic tricks and acrobatics, while simultaneously reaching into their pockets and purses. He pauses, perking his ear slightly when he hears the old truck roll up on him and then suddenly bolts away, disappearing behind the crowd.

From inside the truck cab, they watch as Casey nimbly darts away down the narrow street and around the corner. Rollie stomps on the gas pedal and the rear truck tires bark, leaving dark, rubber skid-marks on the pavement. "Hold on!" The truck lunges forward and rattles around the corner down the uncurbed lane. Jon puts both hands forward to brace on the dashboard and inquires, "Who's the kid? Is he yours?"

The engine growls as the truck races down the alley, not far behind the swiftly-running youth. Rollie speaks aside to Jon as he focuses on navigating the dumpster-lined path. "Casey Kettles, at it again. When I catch hold of 'em this time, I'm gonna kill that little cigar-roller." Casey ducks off through a pedestrian walkway and Rollie continues down to the corner, making a hard, skidding turn at the next street.

The truck roars ahead, buzzing by trees and houses at a speed most likely exceeding the neighborhood limit. Jon looks past Rollie, behind the steering wheel, and sees the long-legged kid dashing between houses and leaping yard fences. Their common eye-line connects a brief moment until Casey skillfully ducks away and disappears again. The truck skids around another corner and Jon holds onto the door handle to keep from sliding across the bench seat.

Jon looks nervously at the determined driver of the truck and mutters, "I don't think you can catch him."

Rollie grips the old truck's steering wheel tighter and pushes the gas pedal hard to the floorboard. "I'll catch him, alright." The truck barrels down another quiet avenue and swerves into a tree-shrouded pathway. To Jon's surprise, Casey appears abruptly, and the truck skids to a screeching halt, pinning a trash can to a line of fencerow, blocking the teen's escape.

Engine still rumbling, Rollie slaps the gear-shifter into neutral and charges out the creaking door. The sunglass-clad youth quickly looks behind for a possible escape and decides to hold his ground. "Hey there, Roland… How ya been doin'? Sure didn't know it was you in that piece of crap ride."

Rollie grabs the slender boy's arm and guides him gruffly toward the truck door. "The hell you didn't... Get in."

The driver's door hangs wide, and Casey slides in behind the wheel. He stops and looks Jon over with curiosity. Casey turns back to Rollie who stands blocking the door, about to get in. "Uh, Roland... Who's the mainlander?"

"Scooch over. He's a friend of Fulton's."

The kid makes a sudden effort to exit the truck and Rollie nudges him back in. Casey shakes his head, grips the steering wheel and refuses to shift along the bench seat. "Fulton? I don't want anything to do with a friend of his!" Rollie shoves the kid over to the middle of the truck seat and slides in behind the wheel. Casey straightens his damp shirt, gives his perspired armpits a quick sniff and looks to Jon. "Hey buddy, you sure have a poor selection of friends."

Rollie glances over at Jon and then at the skinny teenager between them. The street-wise kid sneers and pushes up his yellow-rim sunshades. "Wanna go for a ride, *honey*?"

Rollie glances at Jon, laughingly groans and pulls the truck door shut with a slam. "Don't pay any attention to him. He's what folks around here would call a misguided youth." The engine grinds into gear, and Rollie backs the pickup truck away from the trash can-lined pathway.

Casey turns to look from Rollie to Jon, then back to Rollie again. "Whom do I owe the pleasure of my company?"

The truck whines backwards across the street and stops short of a palm tree stump. Rollie clenches his jaw and stares at young Casey Kettles. "Zip it kid. I'll ask you the questions." He slaps the engine into first gear and the old truck lunges forward down the street.

XIII

The old pickup drives through a serene neighborhood and the three sit shoulder-to-shoulder in the crowded truck cab. Jon sneaks a glance at the awkward-looking pubescent kid seated alongside and wonders why they chased him down. The youth gazes over at Jon above his yellow-rimmed glasses, his gaze darting away when their eyes unexpectedly connect. Jon moves the wet vest at his feet nearer the door to give the boy's spindly legs a bit more space and asks him a question. "Why is it that you don't like Scott Fulton?"

Rollie glances aside as he drives. "The kid was joking."

Casey rolls his eyes over at Jon again and casually pushes up the sunshades on his nose. "No, I wasn't."

Rollie prods the boy with an elbow, and Casey winces. "Quit the nonsense, kid. What were you doing back there?"

Casey responds to Rollie with a snide comment as he takes a probing gander at Jon. "I was helping those people."

Rollie glares at Casey next to him on the truck bench. "Sure looked like you were helping yourself to their stuff." With an irreproachable shrug, Casey sits quietly in his seat as Rollie continues. "You're not a six year-old child anymore, and it just ain't cute. I ought to drive you to the pound and have you arrested."

Casey mockingly offers an innocent puppy face to Jon. "Isn't it sweet that he takes the time to care for poor orphan children like me?" He turns to Rollie on the driver's side. "Sorry to ruin your big important bust, Rolland, but I don't have anything on me."

Irritated, Rollie clenches his jaw tighter as he drives. "We could check out that alleyway back there."

"Don't you old men, dry-farts have bigger fish to fry … like hunting pirates?"

Casey crosses his arms and stares ahead smugly, as Jon, flabbergasted, looks at him. "What do you know about it?"

The street-smart kid flashes a cunning grin and darts his eyes over to Jon. "Not much, but for a nice price I might?"

Rollie turns the steering wheel of the truck and jabs Casey in the ribs again. "Forget it, you little shyster. We're not paying you squat. You're the one in trouble here."

Casey turns his head to peer at Jon and half-whispers, "Rollie is still mighty sore at me about borrowing his truck awhile back."

Shifting on the bench, Rollie grumbles in annoyance. "He took it on a joyride to Miami, then left it, out of gas, on the highway." He grips the truck's steering wheel and frowns. "If I didn't feel damned sorry for your skinny ass, and you weren't Giselle's kid…"

"I know, I know, you'd kick my ass straight."

He casts a paternal glare over at Casey and growls, "Watch your language, kid!"

Island Stepping with Hemingway

Casey shrugs and pushes up the sunglasses on his nose again. "I meant *backside*."

Rollie nods. "Somebody sure needs to."

The wise-ass kid turns to Rollie, squares his shoulders and blatantly smirks in reply. "But are you the man to do it?"

The pilot grips the steering wheel with white knuckles and can barely keep himself from strangling the smart-aleck kid. He stops the truck on the side of the street, swings the door wide open and steps out. He motions for Casey to exit. "We don't have time for this today. Get out!"

Casey slides along the cracked bench seat and mock salutes. "Yes, sir! Thank you, sir!"

Sitting at the edge of the driver's seat, the adolescent lingers and takes off his cheap sunglasses to clean the lenses with the bottom edge of his ratty shirt tail. Rollie grabs him by the collar, yanking him the rest of the way from the truck cab. He leans close, almost nose to nose with Casey. "If I ever find you doing that sort of thing again, I won't take you to the hoosegow, but you'll wish I had."

Rollie releases Casey and slides back into the old truck. The kid smooths out the rumpled neck of his shirt and puts on his yellow rim sunshades. He jumps a step back as the truck door swings shut, and he jeers at Rollie behind the wheel. "Oooh, sometimes you're just like an actual father to me."

Casey grins as he tosses a wristwatch across the cab of the truck to land on Jon's lap. He points a finger like a gun at the two inside and makes clicking noise as he winks broadly. "Welcome to the islands, writer-man. Here's a gift for you." The kid quickly turns on his heels and jogs down the street.

Rollie looks to his empty wrist resting on the steering wheel, then over at the stolen timepiece as Jon inspects it. "That little turd! Give me that."

The irritated pilot takes the pilfered wristwatch and straps it back on, while Jon looks to his own expensive timepiece. "Wonder why he didn't try to swipe mine?"

Rollie grunts, "Oh, he definitely had his beady little eyes on it. Watch out." The duo in the truck exchange a comical look and Jon chuckles as Rollie puts the truck in gear.

~*~

The old truck pulls up to the Key West Marina where a muscle bound, dark-skinned Cuban man washes a vintage 1960's Cadillac. Rollie rolls the truck to a stop and parks a short distance away while gesturing over toward the shirtless thug polishing the classic automobile. "That's Jorgé there detailing the Caddie and Carlos has a boat in slip nineteen." Rollie points his hand over the steering wheel at the luxury yacht backed into the docking slip.

Jon studies the gleaming, two story cabin cruiser, with "Anastasia" across the stern. "Does he live on that thing?"

"Naw, he's got a nice apartment setup across the street from the Conch Tavern, but his base of operations is here." Rollie motions to the item at Jon's feet. "Grab that life vest." Jon pulls the damp item across his lap, and the seaplane pilot nods to the bullet-damaged combat jacket. "If shit goes bad, and I give you the signal, put that thing on quick."

Jon looks at Rollie amazed, "You're kidding! Really?"

Rollie lets out a laugh as he swings the door open. "Naw, just trying to throw in a bit more excitement for you." Jon glances down at the blood-stained, military jacket with the bullet-hole ripped canvas below the armor plating and sighs… "This whole thing has been exciting enough for one day."

Stepping out of the vehicle, Rollie waves him along and lets the driver's side door swing shut with a creaking bang. "Let's see if we can get an audience with the Royal Cuban." Jon follows Rollie toward the parked Cadillac at slip nineteen.

XIV

At the Key West Marina, Rollie and Jon casually approach the private pier, and the large Cuban henchman steps before them to purposely block the way. "Where ya think ya goin'? You got an appointment, Rollie?" Jorgé stands bare-chested before them, flexing his bulky pectoral muscles, dwarfing the physiques of both visitors.

The pilot looks up at the hulking thug with the car rag and offers a friendly smile. "Hey, you big gorilla! Carlos in?"

The oversized bodyguard looks unamused by the comment as he turns his hard stare from Rollie over to Jon. "Who's the puff-tart with the floaty?"

The pilot continues to put on his innocent-looking appearance and makes an effort to step around the wall of muscle. "He's a writer I want to introduce to your boss."

"Carlos ain't in. Come back tomorrow."

"What's your problem today, big guy?"

Jorgé glares down at the uninvited guests and slowly flexes his biceps, as he raises his enormous clenched fists. Rollie grins harmlessly and raises his open palms in surrender. "Easy there, fella. We aren't even in a similar weight class."

"How about I finish the job of rearranging your face?"

"Now, what kind of talk is that between old friends?"

Jorgé grunts like a primate and flares his nostrils. "Don't you be putting on a show at being my friend."

"Who's play-acting?" Rollie graciously extends one of his hands for a diplomatic handshake, and Jorgé attempts to swat it away. The seaplane pilot dodges the awkward swipe with an amused chuckle. Upon missing his intended target, the peeved bodyguard crinkles his heavy brow and ineptly strikes out with his other scrunched fist in a wide-arcing, roundhouse punch directed at Rollie's head.

The amateur boxer nimbly ducks under the swing, jabbing out with his own balled fist into Jorgé's bare abdomen while moving in closer. With a smooth grabbing twist and sidestep, Rollie rotates one of the man's large, muscle bound arms around behind him and pushes him forward over his extended leg. The hefty guard slams to the pavement, and Rollie braces his knee into his spine to keep him pinned there. The bodyguard struggles and winces. "Gol-dammit, Rollie!"

The smaller fighter holds the defender's twisted arm behind his back and nudges the hand further upward to the shoulder blade. "We need to talk with Carlos."

"Screw you flyboy."

The seaplane pilot gives the twisted arm another tweak and Jorgé whimpers in pain. An accented voice from on high at the rear deck of the boat calls out to grab their attention. "That's quite enough, Mister McKinny. Is there something or other I can do for you?" Jon and Rollie both gaze up to see the

Island Stepping with Hemingway

Cuban-imported personage of Carlos Murietta, dressed in his casual occupational attire, leaned on the upper-deck rail of his pleasure yacht.

The overlooking presence stares out from behind an exhaled cloud of cigar smoke. Taking the fat wad of rolled tobacco from his mouth, he lifts a sandaled foot to the railing. He waves the surrounding white haze of smoke away with a swirl of his wrist and salutes with the lit cigar in hand. "You've brought me a visitor?"

The swarthy Cuban entrepreneur is dressed in Caribbean island clothing that rides the fine line between grungy and runway stylish. His slicked-back, dark hair with streaks of gray, along with his olive-skinned complexion, gives him the appearance of an international ambassador to the islands. The fat, rolled Cuban cigar goes to his lips once again for a series of puffs followed by a Cheshire grin, which flashes pearly white and opens many doors of opportunity.

The pilot releases his holding grip on Jorgé and steps away from his possible reach. "No hard feelings big guy?"

The bodyguard brings his twisted arm around to the front and sits, rubbing his sore shoulder. "Screw you, Rolland. If I ever get in the ring with you, I'll knock yer head clean off."

"Fair enough, ya big brute." Rollie steps back next to Jon to get a better view of the man on the boat's upper deck. "How's business, Carlos?"

Jorgé climbs to his feet, holding his aching shoulder while glaring daggers at Rollie. He bends to pick up the dropped carwash towel and keeps silent, as he looks to Carlos. The business-minded figure waves off his sullen henchman and speaks to the two unsolicited visitors. "Fine... Business is fine, Rollie. Who is your compadre there?"

Jon gazes up from the muscled bulk of the bodyguard and introduces himself. "Jon Springer, I'm a friend of..."

"Fulton. Yes, yes… I've heard he's come up missing."

Rollie keeps a vigilant eye on Jorgé and taps Jon on the arm. "Show him the life vest."

Jon steps forward and holds up the military surplus item. Carlos takes a long puff on his cigar, blows out and waves the wand of tobacco through the white cloudy haze. "No, thanks. I see it has a hole in it."

Rollie frowns, as he stares up at the evasive foreigner. "Where's it from, Carlos?"

"It's Cuban. But, you knew that already."

Carlos tilts his head and wags his chin in mock sadness. "Tsk, tsk… You bring this to me because I am the only real Cuban you know… How sad."

The pilot looks to the military vest in Jon's hands and back up at Carlos. "We'd like to find out who it belonged to."

Carlos looks down at the pair of visitors and rolls the cigar between his fingertips. He contemplates a second, then speaks. "You should ask the body that goes with it."

Jon remains respectfully silent, as Rollie continues his elusive banter with the crafty Cuban. "Is there one?"

"Why shoot at an armored vest if there is no one in it?"

Jon examines the bullet-tear in the side of the vest, looks warily to Jorgé and can't help but utter the obvious question toward Carlos. "Can you tell us anything about it?"

Carlos takes a long puff on his cigar and exhales a silvery stream of smoke. "Hmm… Nope."

Rollie rolls his eyes, annoyed at the lack of progress. "Thanks for your help. I hope to return the favor someday." The pilot tilts his head toward the truck as he taps Jon's arm.

As they turn to walk away, Carlos pipes up. "The Cuban military doesn't use that specific style anymore. They don't sell them either." Carlos takes a quick drag on the cigar and exhales. "The Russians supplied them once upon a time, and they were issued strictly to ranking officers." Carlos taps the stacked ash from his cigar over the railing and watches as the flakes drift downward to the water's surface. He stands, catching the afternoon sun. "Thank you for the impromptu social call, Señor Springer. See you around, I suppose."

They stand on the pier and watch as Carlos, with a waving gesture, continues to smile ambiguously while he retreats, disappearing into the upper quarters of his pleasure yacht. Jon holds the life vest at his side and shakes his head. "That seemed pointless. What now?"

"Let's get a drink."

"Will that help us find Fulton?"

The pilot shrugs as he gazes out across the marina. "You never know what might turn up at the Conch Tavern." As they step back toward the truck, Rollie tips a friendly salute to Jorgé, who only scowls. "See ya, big guy." The bodyguard flexes his chest muscles and watches silently, as the two get into the old pickup truck.

From the shadows of the marina storage sheds just beyond, another set of probing eyes observe, as the rusty truck backs up and then drives slowly away from the wharf.

XV

The Conch Republic Tavern is filled with all sorts of types, from guiding fishermen to neighborhood locals and tourists. Rollie and Jon sit in a booth to the back of the room with a full glass of beer before each of them. Jon gazes out to the roomful of mismatched personalities. "Was Carlos any help at all?"

Rollie takes a sip of beer, and a smile crosses his lips. "He's a curious cat, that one. We just needed to plant the seed of intrigue, and he'll find things out."

Jon wraps his hand around his cool pint of poured beer. "What kind of things can he find out?"

Rollie gazes around the room and lowers his voice. "He's got some interesting connections in Cuba, both high up and with the revolutionaries. The trick is to get the information out of him." He nods over to Angie serving drinks to customers at the bar. "She's usually the best way."

Rollie puts on a snarky grin. "He's got a real thing for Angie, but he mostly annoys the piss out of her."

From behind the bar, Angie notices them both looking in her specific direction. She finishes serving a pair of mixed cocktails and moves out into the barroom, approaching the two in the back booth. "Are you two whispering about me?" They simultaneously gaze up at her and can't help but admire her fine, womanly curves, as she takes an authoritative stance at the end of the table. She meets their appreciative gaze and adjusts the damp bar towel hanging from her front belt loop. "Find out anything new about Scott?"

Rollie fiddles with the coaster under his glass on the table and then takes a drink to avoid eye contact with Angie. "Nope, not much to speak of."

She notices Rollie's reluctant reaction to her inquires. "Nothing was spotted from the air this afternoon?"

Attempting to be helpful, Jon chimes in. "We found a life vest with a..." Rollie's foot kicks over to Jon's shin under the table, and the writer lets out a tiny yelp.

Jon gawps across the booth to see a wide-eyed, head-tilted signal from the pilot to keep the information quiet. Rollie coughs to disguise his warning and looks up at Angie. "Probably just a bit of ocean trash and nothing too special." Rollie has another long drink of beer and gestures toward Jon's mostly-full beverage. "Bottoms up, ol' boy. I have to get back and load up for an early fishing trip tomorrow."

Jon stares at Rollie questioningly from across the booth, as he realizes the pilot's sudden urgency to be leaving. He lifts his glass and tips it back and Rollie slides out to get to his feet. After a few gulping swallows of beer to empty his drink, Jon looks to Rollie standing alongside Angie prepared to head for the door. "Why the sudden rush?"

Island Stepping with Hemingway

Rollie ignores Jon's remark and flashes a grin to Angie. "Put 'em on my tab."

Angie sways her curved hip into Rollie's side and raises an eyebrow toward him. "They might as well be on Scott's tab, as good as you two are about paying them."

The pilot wraps his arm around Angie's shoulder. He looks to Jon, still seated at the booth, and tilts his head again toward the exit. "Shake a leg Springer. Time to go."

The confused writer exchanges a friendly look with Angie and hurries to follow the pilot outside. Across the street at the truck, Jon catches up with Rollie and circles around to the passenger side. Across the rusted pickup hood, he gawks at his recent associate and utters, "What was that all about?"

The seaplane pilot swings the door open with a loud creak and slides inside the truck cab. Rollie motions for him to come closer and Jon pokes his head in the open side window. "You need to play the cards closer to the vest back there."

Confused, Jon leans down on the door. "She's the one who sent me to you."

"Not from her exactly, but everybody else in that room. I know about half the characters in there." Rollie looks over his shoulder toward the entrance to the tavern and back. "They're all sketchy and suspicious enough, let alone the ones I don't know." Rollie closes the door with a bang, settles into the bench seat and glances over at Jon. "This island is full of listening ears and desperate folks who will sell out their crippled mother or baby sister for a fast buck or brew."

"Is there anything else we can do?"

The truck cranks, then starts up with a grumbling roar, and Rollie puts his hands on the steering wheel. "Not tonight. I have a fishing trip scheduled in the morning. Should be back by midday… two o'clock. We'll go another round with Carlos then, and see what we've got."

"You think he might be more of a help tomorrow?"

Rollie feathers the accelerator pedal to keep the old rattling engine running. "Bad news travels fast here, and the people in the know always seem to find things out somehow."

Jon pushes back from the window and nods to Rollie. "Thanks for your help today."

"Fulton is a friend. You want a ride home?"

Jon takes a step back from the truck and onto the curb. "I'll walk. I'm only a few blocks away."

Rollie offers a wave and shifts the pickup into gear. "See you on the morrow."

The old truck's headlights flicker on, as it rolls forward into the street and rumbles away. Jon stands and listens to the timeworn vehicle clank and groan, as it rolls around the street corner and fades away into the twilight sounds of the island. Spotting a patch of evening sky through a break in the trees, Jon sighs from the exertion of the day's events.

"Yeah ... he was a good friend."

~*~

The western horizon beyond Key West glows with the last fading colors of sunset. Jon enters the carriage house apartment and lets the screen door spring closed behind him. Through the shadows he reaches to turn on a light and a table lamp switches on spontaneously. The ominous, piratical features of Jacek materialize suddenly out of the darkness.

In shocked surprise, the newly-arrived tenant stares at the undesirable caller. Unmoving, the two lock eyes until Jacek's arcing fist swings out. The blow connects with Jon's temple and tumbles the writer back to the edge of the entry. Jon slowly sinks to the floor, as Jacek's lamp-lit shadow steps past and drops a note on his slumped body. The last thing Jon hears is the departing footsteps of the visiting pirate, as they descend the metal stairway and exit out the back alley gate.

XVI

The single illuminating lamp in the garage apartment slowly comes into focus, and, with an agonizing moan, Jon rolls over. He blinks his eyes several times, struggling to clearly see the hazy nighttime image of a young, sunglass-wearing face. Attempting to look up to the room's beamed ceiling, Jon recognizes the features of Casey Kettles, staring back at him. The adolescent boy assesses Jon lying sprawled out on the floor near the door and grimaces. "I was sent to warn you."

Jon reaches up to touch the throbbing lump on the side of his head and winces. "Thanks..." The young face of Casey begins to distort into darkness, and the ringing pulse of Jon's heartbeat fills his ears. Laid out in the entryway, Jon's eyes roll upward, and the room spins to a whirling vision that fades into oblivion.

~*~

Midair over the waters of the wharf, Scott Fulton's sailboat, *The Fighting Lady,* hangs suspended. A rolling staircase sits positioned at the edge of the dock, next to the dripping, barnacle-free hull. Several trickles of water stream steadily from bullet holes just below the waterline. The dangling ship rocks slightly, as the thumping sound of something inside is heard.

Emerging from below the main deck, Detective Lyle appears blank-faced and empty-handed. His eyes scan the shiny-lacquered top deck for anything out of place or askew. Deep scratches along the finished rail on one side catch his attention and he smooths his hand along the gouged surface. From the corner of his eye he notices something creating a slight bulge under a neatly piled coil of ropes.

The stone-faced detective prudently makes his way across the ship's deck as the whole vessel gently sways on the supporting cables. Detective Lyle looks out over the shipyard, then taps the pile of stacked rope with his foot and nudges the top layers away. He reaches down, pulls the found object free and a faint grin crosses his features.

The detective peers down to the curious discovery in his hands. He scans across the deck of the sailboat again and seems satisfied with his find. There is a distinct clicking, gun-sound as he pulls back the exposed hammer on Scott Fulton's World War I-era six-shot Smith & Wesson revolver.

Familiar with all varieties of firearms, the detective turns the antique pistol over to look at the markings and then presses his thumb to the side release-tab to open the cylinder. The fluted cylinder drops out from the side of the handgun to reveal five brass cartridges, with one having a dented primer. The police detective ejects the cartridges into his hand and counts the four intact bullets and one empty shell casing.

~*~

Island Stepping with Hemingway

The morning sun has risen to shine through the tall palm-leafed trees hanging over the carriage house apartment. Jon sits on the rattan sofa with an iced washcloth pressed to the swollen lump on his sore temple. His head tilted back, Jon gazes blankly out at the view from the front windows, seeing nothing in particular. Then he looks down at the thick piece of card-stock paper resting on his lap.

He opens the folded notecard again and stares at it bewildered as his eyes scan the words. A painful look of dismay consumes Jon's features, as he folds the delivered ransom demand and sets it aside on the phone table. With a crunching roll of ice cubes, Jon adjusts the cold pack on his temple and murmurs aloud, "That's a lot of money."

The shrill ringing of the telephone breaks him from his musings, and Jon turns to the vintage apparatus next to him. The out-of-date communication device rings loudly again and Jon scoops the handled receiver from the cradle phone-base. Before Jon can utter a single word, the extremely identifiable, but faraway sounding voice of his Los Angeles literary agent, C. Moselly, is heard on the other end of the phone line. "Jonny, baby! How are you? Not getting too settled in, I hope. How's the weather down-under, Mate?"

"Oh, it's you, Moselly?"

"Who were you expecting to ring you up with a great book deal opportunity? I'll tell you what's really hot now – *Reality Publication*. That's right, all you have to do is invent a half dozen personalities, pretend they're real people, put them together and make up what happens."

Jon's eyelids flutter as his gaze rolls upward and to the side while he moves the iced bundle to the front of his head. He sighs and asks the obvious question: "And how is that any different than writing realistic fiction?"

"It's all in the repackaging, Mate. Don't they even have cable television down there yet?"

Jon shakes his head at the literary agent's attempted use of an Aussie accent. "I'm not in Australia, so you don't have to call me 'Mate' anymore."

Moselly's voice becomes much louder and clearer, as he picks up the phone receiver and takes Jon's call off speakerphone. "So, you're back in Los Angeles and ready to get to work?"

"I'm still in Florida."

"When did you get there?"

"I'm in the Keys."

There is a slight pause until Moselly pipes up again. "The only keys I am familiar with are the ones to my Porsche collection and Alecia the singer." An expression of perpetual annoyance comes over Jon's features, as he holds the ice pack at his forehead and responds to his agent on the telephone. "What did you want to talk at me about, Moselly?"

"How's my idea sound, Jonny boy?"

"What idea?"

"The non-fiction, make-believe stories I mentioned. You can do your serious novel writing stuff on the side, and we're all back in business."

Jon touches the ice pack to the edge of the sore spot alongside his red, swollen face. Unimpressed, he scrunches his puffy eye painfully and grunts into the old telephone receiver. "I'm working on a bit of reality material right now."

"That's wonderful, Jonny! Great minds think alike! When can I have some pages?"

Jon turns his head aside and gazes at the folded ransom note on the table by the phone. "When I get something together, I'll let you know."

Island Stepping with Hemingway

"Great, Jon! That's just super fantastic! Gotta go now. I'm on my way to the gym to pump some iron and check out the ladies in spandex. Talk to ya soon. Ciao!"

Jon takes the telephone from his ear, reaches over and drops the corded handset on the base. He lays his head back on the top edge of the sofa and stares up at the carved wood palm leaf-shaped blades of the spinning ceiling fan. He sighs heavily, as his eyes flutter closed.

XVII

On the porch landing at the top of the stairs to the garage apartment, Jon exits the screen door and lets it slam behind. High along the left side of his temple, the beginnings of a purple half-moon shiner defines the outer rim of his eye. Touching his swollen face gingerly, Jon looks out past the main house, steps down the spiral stairs to the gardens below and walks out the front gate.

The folded ransom note in hand, Jon appears uneasy and deep in thought, as he travels down the street toward the wharf and marina. Suddenly, the rattling clank of a fully decked-out beach cruiser bicycle careens past him on the sidewalk, nearly knocking him over. The dark-tanned man on the banana-style buddy-seat pedals by at a steady clip, as a fine-looking Macaw parrot clings to his shoulder while squawking and flapping its brightly-colored wings.

The bike-riding pair whooshes past in a blur of motion and Jon stands entranced by the island attraction. "What the heck was that?" Momentarily distracted from his worries, Jon witnesses the flamboyant display of gaudy bicycle-bling and flapping feathers as it continues down the sidewalk, then disappears around a parked van in the street.

~*~

The Key West Historic Seaport is filled with sailboats and charter fishing vessels of all makes, utilities and sizes. Looking the various watercrafts over, Jon walks the docks of the marina. He pauses and gawks at the salvage shipping crane which suspends Fulton's sailboat just above the water. The stark image of the exposed keel makes Jon reflect on the below-the-surface activities and secrets of his longtime friend.

At the end of the marina pier, the exotic man on the cruiser bicycle sits watching, with the parrot on his shoulder and one arm hanging from the high, ape-hanger handlebars. Jon walks toward the enigmatic onlooker, who seems to be outfitted in an assorted style of hippie-homeless-hipster chic.

As Jon approaches, the cagy islander on the bicycle watches, until Jon utters a hesitant greeting. "Hello there."

"Hallo' der, yerself. You da friend of Scott Fulton?

Jon stands before the conch native and can smell a strong musk of patchouli oil mixed with body odor and unwashed seawater. He nods to the peculiar cyclist and gestures over his shoulder at the sailboat, hung high and dry. "Do you know about Scott Fulton?" Jon senses the islander's scrutiny and continues. "Who are you... Did you follow me?"

"I's Aston... Man 'bout town 'n keeper of tales."

Jon touches the tender discoloration around his eye socket, as he studies the mysterious figure seated on the bling-twinkling bicycle before him. The two stare at each other silent until Jon tucks the ransom note in his pocket and questions, "Do you know who visited me last night?"

"I sleep most nights."

Extremely curious, and not feeling particularly threatened by the man on the fancy bike, Jon takes a step closer to Aston. "You one of them? Are you a pirate?"

"What makes you think like dat?" Aston glances down to his bike, overly-decorated with found treasure trash of all different sorts, and grins under his whiskers. "Is it de ride?" Jon studies Aston's bejeweled beach-cruiser with its random shiny bits of scrap items attached to every inch of the frame. He assesses the mysterious stranger's homeless island-style and the colorful parrot perched on his shoulder. "Not just the bike and bird exactly, but put on an eye patch, and you'd really look the part."

Aston swipes the lip-whiskers away from his mouth and flashes a toothy smile, as he tilts his head kindly toward Jon. "It must be da weather in da islands."

"So, you're not one of them?"

The friendly smile suddenly fades from Aston's features, as he looks all around and strokes his tangled beard. "I know most what goes on in dees island waters without being part of the problem."

"What do you think is going on here?"

The man shifts his weight on the long bicycle seat and lets his arm fall to his lap from the high-arching handlebar. "You's been selected for a bit o' trouble to help yo'r friend."

"What do you know about it?"

Aston crinkles his eyebrow and squints as he speaks, "Do you's actually have that many clams to shuck?" Instinctively, Jon touches the ransom note inside his pocket. "You know about the ransom?"

Aston nods and appears downhearted, as Jon continues to converse. "You know they're asking for a lot of money?"

"Yes'um, a ransom for the king of high livin'."

"Do I have any choice in the matter?"

"Pay it if ya like. Won't make too much of a difference on da final outcome."

With keen interest, Jon studies the island philosopher's distinctive eyes, pugilist nose and sun-soaked dark features. The lean-muscled frame and hard, callused knuckles show that the local character does more than just ride his fancy bike around town all day. There is the faintest sort of familiarity when conversing with the charismatic native personality. "Aston, is it? You need something in particular, or did you just want to inform me about knowing my situation?"

Aston's friendly demeanor becomes deadly serious as he gestures Jon closer, glances around and lowers his voice, "If you do as they want 'nd rent a boat to take all dat money, it would be a waste of a good boat and possibly yer life."

"They didn't exactly provide an outline for me with a lot of options. I suppose you have some suggestions?"

Aston puts both his hands to the arched handlebars and raises a sandaled foot to casually spin a bedazzled pedal. "You talk to Madame Giselle at da *Clipped Kitty*. She knows deir type and can get a message through to dem."

Jon seems overly wary of the source, but open for any potential options. "What was the name of that place again?"

Aston grins widely, pushes his fancy pedal forward and swings the tail-end of the bike around in front of Jon. "Hop aboard."

Jon looks at the old-school, banana-shaped glitter seat and the high-backed sissy bar loaded with scraggly, stuffed animals and various items of beach-found garbage zip-tied around it. He shakes his head reluctantly and looks off down the marina. "I'd prefer to walk."

The exotic conch islander on the bicycle offers a grim expression and turns his gaze forward to the docks. He waits while the writer indecisively weighs his options, then mutters. "Der is no times for holiday dilly dally... You don't like your friend very much?"

XVIII

The cool temperatures of the island morning give way to the warmer humidity of daytime. Jon, with his feet propped up on pink conch shells mounted above the rusty chain drive, straddles the back portion of the beach-cruiser bicycle seat. Aston, the urban swashbuckler cranks the creaky pedals swiftly and maneuvers effortlessly through the crowded streets as if he was steering a flying carpet.

Just off the main drag of downtown, the bicycle swerves suddenly and Aston jerks the pedals backwards, bringing the wide, rubber tires to a skidding sideways turn. With Jon hanging on behind, Aston rolls his two-wheeled cruiser up in front of an elaborately-decorated house with heavy garden foliage surrounding the wrought iron entrance. A small engraved brass placard above the mail slot reads:

The Clipped Kitty

As the bicycle rattles to a halt, Aston puts his feet down to balance the pair of riders. His passenger eagerly slides off to one side of the long double bike seat to stand firmly on solid ground. Jon glances around the residential setup and down the quiet tree-lined street. "She's a pet groomer?"

Aston smiles a whiskery, concealed grin and toes his jewel-emblazoned bicycle pedals, giving them a playful spin. "You need to reconnoiter inside to experience for yerself." Standing before the yard gate, Jon lifts the latch to open it. Aston gives a sly flit of his wispy eyebrows and puts a sandaled foot to a spinning pedal as it sparkles in the sunlight. "Jest asks for Giselle."

Jon stands at the entry gate as the odorous smells of the island sage linger in his nostrils and the fragrant scent of the flowered gardens beyond beckon him in. He studies the eccentrically-decorated house before him and hears the beach cruiser bicycle rattle down the pavement. Feeling a bit muddled, Jon glances down the street where Aston pedals away and then back to the ornate wrought-iron entrance before him. "What's a clipped kitty?"

Jon passes through the artsy gateway and walks up the cobblestone path to the large, eye-catching front entry doors. He looks for a knocker or ringer and sees a brass bell hanging next to the entryway. Jon reaches over and gives the dangling, braided string a tug, which chimes the bell, loud and crisp.

The wary visitor looks around prudently, as the ringing reverberates through the luxurious, landscaped surroundings. A small, flapped panel, disguised midway in the decorated door, swings open to reveal a set of welcoming lips coming from the dimly-lit interior. "May I be of some service?"

Jon bends down to waist level and peers into the dark, mysterious opening. "Hello, I'm looking for Giselle."

"J.T. Springs?"

Island Stepping with Hemingway

A flush of nerves comes over Jon as he hears his own literary alias addressed to him from the unbeknownst source. Having his alternate writing identity discovered gives Jon a moment of realization that he might be in way over his head. "Uh… Yes, that's right."

"We wondered if you'd come by."

The small, secreted panel, waist high on the door, closes with a snap, and the larger entryway slowly unlocks and cracks ajar, just enough to reveal the diffusely-lit interior. The soothing female voice from inside the moist-smelling, crevasse summons him in. "Come join us, Mister Springs."

~*~

The creaking of reinforced metal hinges echo loudly, as a jail-like cabin door opens in the hull of the buccaneer yacht. A modern-day pirate drags the limp prisoner inside the barren cabin and drops him to the shiny, polished-metal floor. The bloody, disheveled figure of Scott Fulton rolls over and appears to be the recent casualty of a brutal interrogation. Fulton painfully looks up at his captor through beaten and blood-smeared features. "Why don't we just get it over with?"

The mercenary pirate crewmate stands intimidatingly in the hatch doorway and sneers. "You've had first blood. Now he takes you personal." The brutal figure steps back out of the cabin, and the windowless, metal door creaks closed. After the door slams shut, a fastening latch on the exterior is secured into place, sealing Scott Fulton into silent darkness.

XIX

Jon sits in the entry parlor of the fancy abode that seems a mix between Moorish revival styles and New Orleans Victorian. To shade the remaining outside-light that filters through the dense tree canopy, the windows all have sheer coverings. Alone in the receiving hallway, seated on a red velvet settee, Jon waits, enduring the silence, as he looks around the lavish furnishings and erotic wall-art.

He strains his ears to hear any sound from the home and finally makes out the soft pad of feet on the wood floor. An ethereal female figure glides out from one of the curtained doorways. The dark-haired beauty, with a copper complexion, stands before Jon. He rises to his feet upon her entry and eyes her fine silken robe. In greeting, long feminine fingers extend from inside the flowing sleeve of patterned flowers, and Jon respectfully reaches out his own hand. "Hello, I'm..."

"I know who you are, Mister Springs. I am Giselle."

Jon catches a glimpse beyond, to a shadowed figure moving soundlessly past the doorway and down the hall. After they exchange a kindly handclasp, Jon lowers his arm to feel the cool sensation of mint on his palm. He holds his hand nervously at his side and can't help but observe Giselle's striking beauty, almost forgetting why he is there.

Her tender voice seems to break him from his daze. "Something always comes to pass whenever Scott Fulton returns to our tiny island hideaway. He is a mischievous soul, but most certainly a kind-hearted one."

"Is there something you can do to help my friend?"

"Scott Fulton is more than just a friend to all of us here. I can relay a message and hopefully help out in some way."

"What kind of message?"

Giselle seems to float across the room to where she peels back one of the sheer-covered windows. The soft sunlight dances on her features, as she gazes to the gardens. "They already know who you really are and the full measure of your bank accounts." She looks out and strikes a pose as if someone was observing her from the street and continues. "What they don't recognize is that you have many friends, unbeknownst, here on the island."

"I do?"

"A good friend of a generous soul will take you far."

"I just don't know what you could do to help?"

"You have no idea how the flowing current of friendship works around this island." The desirable woman turns from the sun-filtered window to her visitor and seems to evaluate him for the first time since their brief introduction. Her sensual gaze gleams and dances over him, as she smiles and nods. "I will arrange for something and let you know." She flicks the sheer curtain back with a sweeping motion of her arm, and the room falls dim.

Island Stepping with Hemingway

The two are silent a moment as Jon stands, uncertain of the next step. He stands before Giselle and observes her calm peaceful demeanor. Finally, he lets his nervous stare travel to the front doorway and mutters, "Thank you."

"When you see him, tell Scott... Oh, never mind."

Jon stands in the entry hall and lets his eyes wander the parlor again, feeling the uncomfortable sensation of being secretly watched. He follows after Giselle, as she flows in her robe toward the double wooden doors and unfastens the bolt-latch to one side.

"Good luck to you, Mister Springs." Her cat-like eyes dance playfully, as a smile crosses her lips.

Jon raises his arm to shake hands farewell, but, unsure of himself, hastily drops it, as his sweated palm activates the cool feel of mint again. "Thank you for all your help, I think." Jon connects his gaze with hers, then turns to cross the alluring threshold and steps outside. The door softly closes at his heels, and the chatter of birds in the trees is almost deafening compared to the soundless void of the home's interior. Jon glances back as the ornate door is secured behind him, then walks along the cobblestone path and out the yard gate to the street.

~*~

In the dimly-lit hallways of *The Clipped Kitty*, several scantily-clad ladies move aside as young Casey Kettles darts past them and exits out the rear service door. He runs past the kitchen windows, through the blossoming gardens and slips through a brushy hole in the property's surrounding fence. Merely one street over from Jon and parallel to his traveled path, Casey Kettles rushes down the sidewalk on a seemingly vital errand.

~*~

The streets of Key West are mostly peaceful and calm during the midday lull. Jon strolls along an avenue off the main drag, quietly pondering to himself, and glances down an alley with the persistent, nagging sensation of being followed. The lurching screech of car tires interrupts his rumination and a freshly washed and waxed, Cadillac convertible swipes past Jon into the alleyway. Jon jolts to a halt and looks at the familiar face of Carlos in the topless car obstructing his path.

The swarthy Cuban sits behind the big, pearly-white steering wheel, with one arm over the passenger headrest. "Hello there, Señor Springer." He flares his trademark grin with choppers to match the automobile's immaculate interior. "Out for a leisurely stroll on this fine afternoon?"

Jon quickly recovers from the shock of the automobile nearly running him down and gawks at the Cuban driver. "What are you trying to do with that thing? Run me over?"

Carlos continues grinning as he flips his wrist with a flouncy wave. "Kind of unsettling, no?"

Jon nods, as he steps back from where the car tires almost drove over his foot. "Uh, yes, it is."

"Your new acquaintance, Rollie, the flying cowboy, does it all the time. That rusty old heap of junk of his has no good brakes either." The Cuban fondly gazes down the long, sparkling front end of the Cadillac to the newly polished hood ornament as he speaks to Jon. "He has tagged poor Jorgé into the fence shrubbery twice." Carlos leans over the bench seat, works the lever on the passenger door and pushes it open. "Get in. I have news that should be most interesting for you."

Jon hesitantly steps around the car door and gets into the automobile. He pulls the sizable door closed, and Carlos cranks the wheel and releases the brake. The car lunges forward over the curb and into the street. The engine rumbles under the hood, as the car floats away on white-walled tires.

XX

Carlos drives the open-topped Cadillac leisurely through the palm-lined residential streets of Key West. Colorfully-painted bungalows and houses with wide, overhanging porches line the avenue, with some homes neatly trimmed and landscaped, while others appear to have returned to the primitive tropics. Carlos pivots in the driver's seat to casually observe Jon, momentarily taking his focus away from the roadway ahead. "Key West was not always this garden paradise of green lawns and pretty gardens."

Jon glances at Carlos. "No?"

The Cuban rests his arm over the steering wheel and points to a well-watered property. "Until the pipeline supply of water arrived from the mainland in the forties, the people here had more important uses for their fresh-captured rain." Jon tilts his head and listens, as Carlos continues his discourse.

"Do you know that business deals between the Florida Keys and the island of Cuba have a very long history?"

Jon turns his gaze, observing the sights. "Free trade?"

"Until that ridiculous embargo, Cuba was practically a part of the Florida Keys." Carlos spits as if the mention of the trade embargo puts a bad taste in his mouth. Several bicycles roll past, and Carlos wipes faint perspiration from his brow.

The car rolls along slowly, and Jon looks over at Carlos. "Hasn't the embargo mostly been lifted?'

"Once you have a strangle-hold on a small country for over half a century, do you merely just let go and expect life will return to normal?" Jon shrugs indifferently and has no choice but to listen to the lecture of the Cuban businessman. "Señor Springer, do you understand that the island of Key West is actually nearer to the nation of Cuba than it is to the United States mainland?" Carlos stares at Jon, and the automobile seems to be steering itself, since the driver isn't paying much attention to the road. "There is just a short stretch of water that divides the two."

The car swings toward oncoming bicycle traffic, and Jon hastily points forward at the cyclists. "Watch the bikes!"

The car swerves, and Carlos twists in the seat to put his attention back to driving before turning toward Jon again. "Historically, the Keys have much closer ties to Cuba than the rest of your country. Did you know that?"

Jon grips the door handle as the car angles toward a row of loaded trash bins. Carlos quickly veers from the lineup, as Jon gapes out the front windscreen of the vintage automobile, getting the sense that this trip is getting him nowhere but is destined for an accident. "That's a nice geographical history lesson, but if you can't help me with my friend, Scott Fulton, I'm a little busy today."

Island Stepping with Hemingway

Carlos glances over at Jon and gives a sassy shake of his slicked-haired head. "I did not just pick you up to chit-chat, Señor Springer. Do you know how long I've been in these Caribbean Islands?"

"Looking at your car, I'd say since the sixties."

Carlos smooths his hands around the steering wheel and nods approvingly. "That is a smart answer, but no."

"How long has it been then?"

"Check the attitude at the door, please."

Jon evaluates Carlos and begins to understand that he gets some sort of pleasure from his little information game. The Cuban glimpses over at Jon with a sly, but obvious, wink. "I lived in Cuba most my life, raised by the Revolution." Carlos turns forward just in time to swerve casually around a gathering of free range chickens pecking across the roadway. "I came to this island of Key West in the early spring of 1982. Do you know what happened then?"

"The Bee Gees did a free concert?"

"No... Whispers of another revolution brought me here. I was sent on a special assignment as a secret emissary to perform the necessary groundwork and support to annex the Florida Keys to the Nation of Cuba."

Jon turns in his seat to Carlos and raises an eyebrow at the far-fetched idea. "How'd that work out for you?"

"Obviously the revolting islanders weren't very serious when they announced their succession from the United States, or they would have become a part of Cuba." Carlos gapes vacantly at blue sky as if remembering his former glory days. A cunning smile crosses his lips as he turns to face Jon again. "I was here to negotiate the deal and sweeten the pot a bit."

Jon tries to make out if Carlos is serious or just fabricating an entertaining story. "You're telling me that Key West seceded from the United States of America in 1982?"

The two exchange a dubious glance, and Carlos resumes his unbelievable tale. "The entire chain of islands actually, from where you have taken up residence, all the way to the southern tip of Florida.

Carlos takes a fat cigar from his shirt pocket and puts it in his mouth. "Angie's grandfather renamed that old tavern after the newly-formed independent republic."

"Conch Republic?"

Carlos rotates the Cadillac's wide steering wheel and drives them down another picturesque, bungalow-lined street. "It was an independent nation for a minute or so."

"You're joking. I've never heard that."

Carlos sighs and stops the car to watch a group of men playing dominoes on a wooden crate along the sidewalk. "Yes, in the early eighties, there was a mass exodus from Cuba and a roadblock was set up on the Florida mainland to block illegals from entering the rest of the United States."

Enthralled by the unusual story, Jon turns in his seat. "Cuban immigrants?"

"Yes... The travel restriction was choking the life out of the local economy of all the islands, so the only recourse they had was to declare their independence from the United States of America." The Cuban storyteller glances over at Jon and notices that the unusual tale has him... hook, line and sinker. "The revolution was short-lived." Carlos waves his palm in the air as he steers with one hand. "Like a silly child's game, they broke a stale loaf of Cuban bread over the head of a man in a U.S. Navy uniform and then surrendered to the Union, demanding one billion dollars in foreign aid."

"A billion dollars?"

Carlos shrugs and rests both his hands on the steering wheel as he drives. "For 'War Relief', to rebuild after the long federal siege. The worldwide press received was influential, the roadblock was finally lifted and all was mostly forgiven." Carlos brakes the auto, turns a corner and steps on the gas. The car zooms forward to no place in particular, then glides. "Anyway, it was all quite embarrassing for me, since I was specially appointed by Fidel, himself."

Under the midday sun, the open-topped convertible cruises through the house-lined streets. With his hand, Jon shields the blinding glare from his eyes and squints at Carlos. "Is that the reason you stay around here and not in Cuba?"

The driver peers over his shoulder and smooths back his slicked hair. "I stay because I choose to. Someday, though, when the time is right, I will be the successor to Castro."

Jon can't help but be charmed by the poised Cuban. "That's quite the bold statement, since his brother just took over the helm."

Carlos turns to Jon with a look of unquestionable confidence. "Yes, yes it is."

"Do you still go back to Cuba?"

"I go back at times. It is not always pleasant, though."

They both gaze around at the surprisingly rural fixtures of the non-touristy part of the island. Domestic poultry and yard-goats predominate, as they continue to drive the less affluent island neighborhoods.

Carlos peers over at Jon and lowly whispers in secret, "I hear you need a boat?"

Jon seems disconcerted that the Cuban businessman already knows of the most recent plans for aiding his friend. Carlos draws a calling-card from the inner pocket of his sport jacket and holds it out for Jon. "Phone this number when you have everything arranged and are in need of our service."

Jon takes the card and looks down at the local number. "What's the catch?"

"What some gentlemen do on the high seas affects what all men do. You take care of your business, and we'll be sure to take care of ours." Carlos drives the old car in front of Jon's new home and eases the large automobile to a halt. "Good day. We'll talk again soon, Señor Springer."

Jon pushes the car door open and steps to the curb. He looks back inside the automobile to Carlos, skeptically. "Anytime I need your boat?"

"Yes... Unless you would want to try and accomplish a sensitive, life or death business deal with that rowdy cowboy in the seaplane?" Amused, Carlos snorts to himself and grins. "Call the number. I'll be around." Jon swings the heavy passenger door closed and the vintage automobile rumbles and slinks off on white, side walled tires. Carlos gives a flipping wave of his hand and drives down the street, as Jon stands in the shade of an overhanging tree.

Seeming to be alone on the quiet avenue, Jon enters the landscape-shrouded front gate of his new residence and walks through the manicured gardens. He ambles up the stairway to the carriage house apartment and heaves an extended sigh of relief, as he steps through the doorway to the cooler interior. Suddenly, Jon feels the sharp unpleasant jab of a pistol barrel being pressed into his ribcage and, with disbelief, grunts, "Now what?"

XXI

From the entryway to the carriage house apartment, Jon is quickly tugged further inside. He is aggressively spun around to be confronted by the first mate, Jacek holding a gun on him. The mercenary pirate points the lethal weapon threateningly, and Jon raises his hands above his head, hoping to calm the suddenly tense situation. "Hey, there… Easy, fella…"

"I don't do things easy."

Jon glances around the carriage house for something to possibly defend himself with and keeps his hands high. "What do you want?"

"Come with me."

"Where?"

"Don't speak, just follow me."

Jacek angrily motions the military-grade handgun and points Jon out through the apartment door. "You do what I say, when I say, and no more wasting time!"

They are about to exit the apartment together when the borrowed jacket from the seaplane flight catches Jon's eye. "Wait, let me grab my coat." He sidesteps the entryway and lifts the rolled bundle from the table.

The mercenary pirate stares at his captive strangely, then looks to his own sleeveless arms and nods his consent. Jon tucks the borrowed Key West Air Charters jacket under his arm and, holding the wrapped content secure, steps to the open door. At the screened entryway, he glimpses back at the angry pirate, sensing the grave situation he finds himself in. Stepping out, Jon is followed closely by the armed gunman.

~*~

After a short stroll they arrive at the Key West Marina and Jon is cautiously ushered along the waterfront docks. Jacek conceals the firearm at Jon's back, as the hostage writer scans the wharf for help. He notices that no one is in sight, despite the mid-afternoon hour and murmurs to himself, "Everyone can't be napping..." The close moving pair walks past Scott Fulton's suspended sailboat and then, farther down, they saunter by the slip where Carlos's yacht sits docked.

Jon peeks over his shoulder at his weapon-carrying escort and attempts to remain calm despite his uncertainty. "Have you considered someone might see us here together?"

Jacek smirks as he scans the wharf. "Who? I don't see anyone around." He pushes the barrel harder into Jon's back, and they walk to a waiting speedboat at the end of the pier.

The mercenary pirate ushers Jon into the watercraft and unties the dock lines. He coils the ropes and tosses them aboard before climbing in behind the controls. Jacek tucks the pistol in his waistband and stares at Jon, who is obviously uncomfortable in his newfound appointment as prisoner. "Relax there, writer-man. We need you for your money, remember."

Island Stepping with Hemingway

The unpleasant observation does nothing to relax the mood, as Jacek starts up the powerful speedboat engines. Water churns from the underwater propellers and drifts them from the dock. A slight push forward on the throttle carries them out of the marina, away from possible hope of rescue. Without a soul to witness their departure, the speedboat is thrust into high gear and churns a deep wake, as it races out to the open waters beyond.

~*~

At the carriage house apartment, Rollie walks up the spiral stairway and raps his knuckles on the screen door. "Springer... Hey Jon, ya in there?" The pilot presses his face to the louvered glass windows next to the doorway and peers inside. He pulls on the handle to the screen door and swings it open with a soft, creaking jangle. "Hello... Springer?"

The garage apartment appears vacant and peacefully quiet, as Rollie scans the interior for Jon. "Anyone at home?" Warily, the pilot moves around the room, noticing the still-packed suitcase in the corner and the notebook computer sitting closed on the table. He goes to peek in the back bedroom and bath area, then returns to the main living space. "I guess I'll be seeing you at the tavern."

Rollie moves to the door and his studious gaze passes over the dust swept spot on the table where his jacket and pistol had rested a short time earlier. Feeling uncertain, he turns back to the apartment and gives it a final once over. With a creaking slam, Rollie finally pushes past the wooden screen door, and his feet are heard descending the metal steps to the gardens below.

A scuffling thump of elbows and knees on the wood floor comes from under the rattan sofa in the living room. Bare skin squeaks against the dusty hardwoods and the face of Casey Kettles peeks out from beneath the seating area.

He sits on the floor and pats himself off with a cough. Crawling on all fours to the window, he watches outside as Rollie exits the yard to the house and climbs into his truck. The old pickup cranks a few times, then starts and rolls away. Casey gazes around the room once more, puts on his yellow-framed sunshades, and slips out the creaking screen door.

XXII

The pirate yacht sits off the shore in the deeper waters near Marquesas Key, halfway to the islands of the Dry Tortugas. Bright blue skies and a tropical setting give a false appearance of leisure. The display of reflective glass panes on the ship's bridge remains dark, looming and quiet. At the stern of the sleek seagoing vessel the muscle-engine speedboat sits tied, bobbing gently in the clear ocean waves.

In the cabin hull of the modern pirate vessel, Jon waits in a holding chamber, seated behind a windowless steel door. Above the door, a lamp with a single bulb shines a bright, white light into the bare room through a protective wire cage. Jon stares down at what appears to be a fresh smear of blood on the polished floor and gets a sick sensation in his stomach. Not feeling much reassurance from the hidden pistol tucked in the pocket of the jacket, Jon shifts the bundle on his lap.

The sound of feet shuffling outside the door arouses Jon's attention and he tucks the coat-wrapped firearm in the narrow space under the bunk. Finally, the door swings open and Jacek appears, gun in hand. The pirate steps into the compartment, flashes a foreboding grin and wags the tip of the gun barrel at Jon. "Come with me. He'll see you now." Reluctantly, Jon stands and follows Jacek out the cabin door. In the dim companionway, they pass by several closed-off rooms and then ascend a set of stairs leading to the bridge.

Upon entering the pirate yacht's main control room, Jon gazes out through the wide panel of dark-tinted windows. A voice from behind startles Jon and draws his attention away from the awesome view of serene seascape. "J.T. Springs?"

Jon turns to come face-to-face with Captain Longley. He looks at the uniformed naval gentleman who is clearly the captain of the ship. "Who are you... Long John Silver?"

Captain Longley gives a pleasant nod and a sly grin. "Very nice makings of a shiner you have there, Mister Springs. You may address me as Captain Longley."

"You bring me all the way out here to apologize?"

"Be careful with your tone, or I may have Jacek inflict you with another to match the one you're already sporting."

Jon impulsively touches the tender contusion high on his cheek and mumbles under his breath to the pirate captain. "Sure, I always wanted to have eyes like Tammy Faye Baker." Captain Longley signals faintly to Jacek, and the mercenary first mate instantly jams his hammered fist into Jon's ribcage. The air knocked from his lungs, Jon crumples to the floor. With painful breath, he looks up at the two pirates standing over him and slowly regains his feet.

Captain Longley waits for Jon to rise and then resumes addressing his guest. "May I have your full attention now?" Jon nods obediently and takes a deep, wheezing lungful of air, as the captain continues. "Hopefully you are not as thick-headed and obstinate as your good pal, Mister Scott Fulton." The captain sniffs and clasps his hands together before him. "We had to mistreat him for hours, before he was sociable."

"What do you want me to do?"

Captain Longley takes a breath and calmly exhales. "You received our note, and I received your countered message from the bordello." He strides to the observation windows, gazes at the nearby mangrove coast and turns on his heel to face Jon. "This is really a waste of everyone's time. There will be no negotiations." The captain stares hard at Jon and accentuates his words. "You deliver the ransom as stated or I'm done with you both."

Jon holds his sore ribcage and glances over hesitantly at Jacek before responding, "Will you release us both now?" Captain Longley shakes his head and touches his sore side. "No, he has caused us too much trouble to just let him go."

Mind racing and feeling sick to his stomach, Jon utters feebly. "Before I pay, I need to know that Fulton is alive."

Captain Longley stands before the ship's main controls and presses one of the buttons on the console. He lowers his chin and speaks into a microphone protruding from the panel. "Put Mister Fulton on. He has a visitor." The yacht's intercom crackles with waves of static, and Jon steps forward to speak. "Scott, are you okay?"

The intercom is unresponsive, until the obstinate voice of Fulton transmits, loud and clear, "Jon, get out of here..."

Captain Longley lifts his finger from the control button to disengage the intercom connection and shakes his head. "Like I said, he is a most thick-headed person. Hopefully you have a bit more sense of the severity of this situation."

Jon glances around the yacht's main command center, then back to the captain standing at the section of windows.

He tries to come up with any ideas to negotiate with that might buy his friend a bit more time. "Captain… How do you think I could get my hands on that much money?"

Annoyed, Longley grunts, "I don't care how you do it."

Jon peeks behind at Jacek and back to Captain Longley. "I could sell Fulton's sailboat and get you that money in cash."

The captain continues to stare out through the section of tinted windows, as he tersely responds to his hostage guest. "Mister *J.T. Springs*, do not attempt to insult our intelligence. You are a widely published mystery and adventure writer. You do receive royalties, do you not?"

Longley casts a sidelong glare at Jon and continues. "Have the demanded amount of money ready and deliver it as instructed, or pick up what is left of Mister Fulton's body from the ocean depths."

At wits end, Jon shakes his head. "Why the ransom? Scott could just write you a check for what you demand."

Captain Longley turns deliberately around to face Jon. His shadowed features possess a grim expression. "I do hope *your* personal finances are in much better order." The captain waits for a telling reaction from Jon, but receives nothing and continues. "Upon inspection, Mister Fulton has overextended his credit on several fronts. That is, on every front, in fact. Most notably of which, he owes me a great deal of reimbursement for which you will have to make recompense."

"You're telling me Scott is broke?"

Captain Longley lets an arrogant grin escape his lips. "Yes, that is a very modest way to put it." Jon pauses to let the shocking information sink in. Finally accepting what has to be done to save his longtime friend, Jon stands a bit straighter. "Where and when do we meet?"

Island Stepping with Hemingway

The captain gestures toward the first mate, and the mercenary henchman hands Jon a GPS device. "We will be sending you instructions."

Jon stares down at the global tracking instrument. Suddenly getting a chilling sense of powerlessness, he utters, "What if I go to the police?"

The captain pivots to his expansive view out the bridge windows, turning his back on the novelist. "I know for a fact that the police could care less about your fellow wordsmith. We should hope you have slightly more concern for his life." Captain Longley waves a gesture to Jacek, and he nods the captive guest toward the exit. Struggling to find the words, Jon bites his lip with frustration. As Jon is ushered to the door, Longley calls out to him. "I hope you won't be thinking of doing anything foolish, Mister Springs... his time is short."

Jacek escorts Jon at gunpoint from the control room, leaving Captain Longley staring out through the tinted row of windows. In the companionway, Jon casts a quick glimpse back through the doorway and catches the dark looming silhouette of the pirate captain against the vast open seascape. Jacek firmly pulls the door closed and shoves Jon forward. "Keep it moving, writer-man."

~*~

The waters on the northern coast of Key West are lively with afternoon activity at the marina and sailing club. Jon sits at the front end of the speedboat as it glides through the busy maritime traffic of fishermen coming in and sailboat tours heading out. He observes the various goings-on and murmurs to himself, "Where was everyone when I was shanghaied?"

Jon glances back at Jacek, who has a gun concealed by a towel and gestures toward the approaching dock. The boat cruises near, Jon steps out and, before both his feet are settled on the wooden deck, Jacek steers the watercraft swiftly away.

An authoritative voice calls from the crowd of sunset cruise tourists to Jon. "Mister Springer, any word from Fulton?"

Jon turns to see Detective Lyle move out from behind several people near the boathouse. He startles at the sudden presence of the police detective and, before responding, quickly attempts to evaluate how long he's been observed. Forcing a smile, Jon shrugs. "No, nothing yet."

The detective looks out across the crowded marina and watches as the high-powered speed boat races to open water. His attentive gaze follows the churned wake and returns to the spot where Jon was hurriedly dropped off at the pier. "Who's your new friend with the fast boat?"

Jon peers over at an unattended tackle box and fishing rod leaned on the boat house wall. "Uh, he took me fishing."

"Didn't catch anything?"

"Not really."

There is a tension-filled silence between the two, as Detective Lyle eyes Jon suspiciously. Lyle tilts his head. "You're either a terrible fisherman or an even worse liar."

"Why would you assume that?"

"This is some of the best fishing in the world out here. Maybe you need some different friends… or different bait."

Lyle narrows a watchful eye, and Jon intuitively understands the island detective's meaning. "Maybe I do."

Detective Lyle wags a warning finger at Jon and then goes to grab the tackle box and fishing rod leaning against the boat house. With fishing gear in hand, he turns back and grins shrewdly. "If you catch anything illegal, we'll nail you for it."

Jon walks to the detective and pauses to contemplate before glimpsing down the pier. Nearly shoulder to shoulder, the two men read the other for any useful bits of information. Jon steps away from the detective and speaks over his shoulder. "I'll let you know if I hook anything I can't handle."

Island Stepping with Hemingway

Jon works his way through crowds of milling tourists. Walking along the boat-filled wharf, he glances over at the police detective still watching him. Detective Lyle curtly waves and calls after him. "You be sure to do that Springer. We're serious about our big fish around here."

XXIII

Throngs of vacationing travelers swarm the streets, spilling out from the souvenir shops and watering holes of Old Town. A loud bell splits the crowd as the *World Famous Conch Train* chugs by. Smiling customers, with cell phone cameras and beverages sloshing from plastic cups, hang over the sides. Gas-powered scooters and bicycles wheel around a stopped rental car attempting to make a left turn across the boulevard, as Jon steps up to the front door signage of a National Bank.

He stares at his mirror image in the door's tinted glass and then at all the busy vacationer activity passing along behind him. The dark reflection on the entry door is a somber reminder of the bridge on the pirate yacht and the ransom demand. Distressing thoughts of the massive amount of money needed to rescue his longtime friend cause beads of nervous perspiration to trickle from Jon's brow. He pushes the lobby door open and receives a blast of cool air full in the face.

~*~

In the carriage house apartment, Jon sits the sofa with the old-fashioned telephone on the coffee table before him. The unused portable laptop computer is still on the writing table next to his leather shoulder bag. He stares at the antiquated calling device, looks to the odd pairing of business cards placed on the coffee table, and then to the lumpy duffle bag at his side, loaded for the ransom delivery.

Reaching out, Jon's hand hovers first over the card with the Key West Police insignia on the upper right-hand corner. He glances again to his writing workstation and murmurs, "What would the illustrious *J.T. Springs* do in this situation?" His hand impulsively moves over to the other calling card and lifts it from the coffee table. Jon shakes his head uncertain and grunts, "J.T. Springs is gonna get your ass killed…"

Jon picks up the telephone's receiver and dials his finger round a succession of numbers on the old rotary base. A tense moment passes as the dial tone turns to ringing, and Jon takes a short, shallow breath. "Hello… Is this Carlos?" Listening a moment, Jon gives a nod, as he looks to the money-stuffed duffle sitting beside him. "We should meet at the Conch Republic? Yes, I know where it is. I'll be there."

The telephone line connection cuts off and drones an empty tone that lingers in Jon's ear. He hangs up the phone receiver and drops the Cuban's calling card to the coffee table's wooden surface. Gazing around the small room, Jon's eyes travel aimlessly, then stop on his laptop computer, still waiting to be used, on the writing table. He puts his face in his hands and mumbles aloud, "Coming up with this stuff on paper is a lot less dangerous than living it."

XXIV

The remarkably heavy attendance of evening bar patrons at the Conch Republic Tavern has made the inside of the saloon hot and steamy. There is a general raucous clamor in the room, backed by local island music coming over the bar speakers. Jon enters the crowded drinking establishment and looks around at the assortment of new and unfamiliar faces.

The room is filled with tropical tunes, tourist good-cheer and general chatter as Jon works his way toward the congested bar. As he continues to examine the diverse crowd, he steps into a heavy-framed, hulking bodybuilder. Jon begins to apologize until he peers up to instantly recognize Jorgé. "Oh, excuse me, there... Where is Carlos?" The Cuban henchman grunts and wordlessly extends a pointed finger, attached to a clenched fist, over Jon's shoulder to a private booth at the back of the bar.

Jon takes a step back, moves around the muscled figure and approaches the booth where Carlos is seated. "Hello?"

"Ahh, Señor Springer..."

Jon stands before the booth and feels the bodyguard come up and take a firm stance behind him. The Cuban businessman gestures to the empty bench seat opposite. "Welcome to my home away from home." Carlos watches keenly, as Jon glances behind at Jorgé and reluctantly slides onto the vinyl bench across from him. "A drink for you?"

Carlos flips a wave to Angie, as she comes out from the stock room with a case of beer. She deliberately seems to ignore the Cuban, until she notices Jon seated at the table. Jorgé moves to a guarding position at the wall and Angie puts what she's carrying down and starts for their booth. Placing his elbows on the table, Jon leans forward to whisper loudly, "So, can I use your boat?"

Carlos puts up a raised, open palm to hush Jon as Angie approaches. "Ahh, darling, could you find it in your warm heart to fetch an adult beverage for my new friend?"

Angie turns her gaze to Jon and wags her head upset. "Jon, as far as new friends, you could do a helluva lot better."

Jon smiles meekly and offers up his only explanation. "Rollie acquainted us earlier, and I'm still finding my way."

"I'll be sure to have a good talk with him about that." The saloon owner puts a hand to the bar-towel tucked at her hip and points the other at Jon. "What'll you have, Springer?"

"One of those Sunset ales would be fine."

"Sure thing, sweetie." Angie turns to Carlos and sighs, "Anything else for you?"

Carlos smoothes his open palms along his slicked hair and beams lovingly over at her. "To cast my undeserving eyes upon your heaven-sent beauty is enough."

Island Stepping with Hemingway

Annoyed, Angie tilts her head and rolls her eyes back. "Save the silky pillow-talk for your gal-pals at Giselle's."

The Cuban observes her departure while letting out a low, purring, tiger-like growl. "She can hardly control herself around my Latin heat."

Jon pulls his own gawking stare from the saloon owner's curvy backside and settles in the creaky vinyl booth. "I don't know… She sorta seemed annoyed."

Carlos deftly snaps his fingers, stares across the table at Jon and winks. "That is just one of the early stages for an enduring passion."

Jon glances around the roomful of differing personality types, then to Angie behind the bar, pouring another drink. "So, you said you could help me?"

"Yes, yes, down to business."

"I have the ransom. You offered your boat service?"

Impressed, Carlos raises a surprised eyebrow at Jon. "You were able to pull the funds together that quickly?"

"It wasn't easy to empty all my accounts in one day."

Jon sighs disheartened and Carlos grunts with a familiar gesticulation of his hand. "No matter. If all goes well, you will retain your accumulated fortune."

The Cuban's words bring little comfort, and Jon replies, "I don't like the, *if all goes well* part of your idea."

Carlos takes a sip from the cocktail glass on the table in front of him and swirls the thin straw in the remaining ice. "Where do they request you make the drop?"

Jon pulls the GPS from his pants pocket and slides it across the barroom table. "This is what they gave for receiving the delivery guidelines."

Carlos nods, as he studies the automated device with its small screen. He turns the electronic gadget over to look at the backside. "Did they give you any other directions?"

"They said to have all the money prepared."

"They? Are you referring to Captain Longley?"

"Is this someone you know?"

"I heard he was around, and we have a history."

"I don't remember if he properly introduced himself."

"Oh, I have heard that is indeed Longley involved." Slightly perplexed, Jon continues to explain and Carlos listens. "The pirate captain said the exchange coordinates are supposed to show on that thing and then to make delivery."

Carlos grins and slides the device with the blank screen across the table to Jon. "Sorta like a fancy restaurant?"

Jon takes the GPS device off the table and tucks it away. "A very expensive restaurant, somewhere in the middle of the ocean, that the very thought of makes you lose your appetite."

Carlos looks to Jorgé positioned against the wall before suspiciously scanning the faces in the room. He whispers low, "Be at the yacht club tomorrow at o-five hundred hours."

"Do you have some elaborate plan?"

Carlos shifts out of his apprehensive demeanor and puts on his game face while finishing the last sip of his drink. "We must prepare for the worst to be at our best in this encounter. To acquire your friend and get yourself out of this alive, it would be advisable to stack the odds in our favor." Jon nods his agreement and watches as Carlos slides out from the booth. He looks down at the global positioning device on his lap, as Angie approaches the table with his drink.

Carlos stands with an exaggerated genuflect to Angie.

"Miss Storm, when will you ever take me up on my generous offer of a romantic getaway?"

Angie crinkles her brow with a grimacing expression. "Just the two of us, eh?"

Carlos grins wide and amenably. "And my man Jorgé, of course, to be of any service to us."

Island Stepping with Hemingway

Angie moves around the groveling Cuban and shakes her head, as she tosses out a coaster and sets down Jon's beer. "I think any romance with you would be like parading around town on the village bicycle with no seat."

Carlos puts on his most endearing charm and leans in to whisper, "Most everyone else has tried it… Why not you?"

With a stiffly-pointed finger to his forehead, Angie pushes the Cuban away and wipes her hand on the bar towel tucked at her waist. "A little too much hair gel must be affecting your brain." Angie backs from their table and tells off Carlos. "I'm not for sale now or ever… neither is my bar."

The flagrant admirer puts on a display of mock offense. "I did not even mention or hint at owning your establishment. I only crave the warmth of your female companionship."

Jon takes a drink from his beer and starts to enjoy the stimulating encounter. Angie slants her gaze down at Jon while trying to disregard the amorous Cuban fluttering his eyelids at her. "You think this is funny? Well, it gets old fast."

With a shrug, Jon takes another sip of his beer and remarks, "Somewhat entertaining." Angie groans and gestures across the crowded barroom to the lineup of occupied stools. "Springer, when you get tired of this one's company, come join me at the bar. I'll buy you a drink."

Carlos stealthily brushes his hand across her exposed midsection, sliding a twenty dollar bill into her pants-waist, just above the hip and playfully smiles. "I was just leaving."

Angie looks down at the obvious stripper tip, removes it and jauntily slides it into her cleavage. "Go on and scram!"

"Ahh, Angie. You know how to drive a lovelorn gentleman crazy with desire."

Angie looks at Jon in the booth, acknowledges Jorgé against the wall and steps past Carlos. "You're so full of it, Carlos. I have to get back to work. See ya tomorrow, I guess."

They watch her swagger away and Carlos whistles low into the loud clamor of the barroom. He turns to Jon excitedly. "She is quite a firecracker, no?" Still seated in the booth, Jon tilts his head and shrugs a shoulder, as Carlos gives a rap of his knuckles on the laminate tabletop.

The zealous Cuban gives a flouncy departing gesture as he follows his hired henchman, Jorgé, across the busy room. Jostled bar patrons are ungracefully shuffled aside by the brawny bouncer. Jon takes another gulping swallow from the beer before him, glances around the crowded tavern and shakes his head in dismay.

XXV

The early light of a new morning is masked by a thick bank of heavy fog hanging over the Caribbean island of Key West. In the predawn hour, Jon descends the stairs of the carriage house apartment with the ransom-loaded duffle bag in hand. He moves along beside of the bottom portion of the multi-car garage and steps out the back alleyway gate.

Walking the quiet street, the solitary, mist-shrouded figure of Jon "J.T. Springs" Springer makes his way to the waterfront and ducks back as a set of car headlights pierce through the haze. From the concealment of a low leafy palm, Jon watches as a Key West Police Jeep cruises slowly down the street and passes just before him. He steps out again to the paved walkway and continues through the misty dawn in the direction of the island marina.

Eric H. Heisner

The soft clatter and thump of boats tied at the docks greets Jon as he walks to the slip where Carlos keeps a yacht. He makes out the luxury vessel's name, *Anastasia*, painted across the transom and peers through the thick moisture hanging in the air, highlighted by a lamp on the boathouse. Jon stands on the pier, before the Cuban's yacht, and begins to have second thoughts about the ambiguous rescue plan.

He looks down at the loaded duffle, filled with the payoff, and abruptly feels a weighty hand upon his shoulder. With a startled cringe, Jon pivots to look straight into the broad chest of Jorgé. The giant henchman grasps Jon's shoulder firmly and speaks quietly, in his thick foreign accent. "Señor Springer?" Jon tries to twist free of the heavy's hold, but the grip is strong. "Yes, I'm Springer."

"Did you come alone?"

"I don't have too many friends here to choose from." Jon feels the tightening squeeze of the large man's grip upon his shoulder and gasps, timidly, "Yes, I'm alone."

Through the hazy brightness cast from the boathouse lamp, Jon can barely make out the guard's shaded features as the big man speaks. "Señor Murietta awaits you on board."

Jorgé ushers Jon forward on the pier alongside the yacht and finally releases his iron-like grip when they reach the gangplank. Massaging the flow of blood back into his tender shoulder, Jon glimpses at the hulking wall of muscle coming behind him. The fleeting thought of diving into the dark harbor crosses Jon's mind, until Jorgé gives him another persuasive shove. Moving up the gangway, Jon steps forward, climbing onto the yacht of the notorious Cuban businessman.

~*~

Inside the anchored pirate yacht, a freed Scott Fulton moves stealthily through the unoccupied companionway, assertively escorting a pirate crewman at gunpoint before him.

Island Stepping with Hemingway

The sullen seaman stops before a door with a small porthole window and hooks a thumb over his shoulder at the entry. "This is the ship's radio communications room."

With a firm grip on the crewman's collar, Fulton keeps the pistol barrel pushed into the man's ribs and peeks in through the small round window. "Good. Now take it easy. You tip off that radioman before I say so, and I'll ruin you."

The crewman turns his head toward Fulton and sneers. "We're near international waters. Who do you think you're going to call… Uncle Sam?"

Fulton jerks the pirate's collar, shoving him toward the door latch. "You might be surprised… I've got friends all over the place."

The pirate murmurs under his breath. "I doubt it."

Fulton twists the gun barrel's tip hard into the pirate captive's spine and nudges him forward. "Just try to be cool, and introduce me to the nice fellow operating the wireless." The door handle turns with a clunking rattle, and the metal hatch swings open. Wearing the *Key West Air Charters* jacket, Fulton prods the pirate crewman with the handgun, and they step through the passageway into the radio control room.

~*~

The sleeping island of Key West is quickly left behind in the dense bank of fog, as the Cuban yacht cruises through the dark, rippling waves of the marina toward open water. The obscured glow of the morning sun is mostly veiled by the overcast weather conditions. Jon stands on the upper foredeck of the foreign yacht, next to Carlos. He lowers a set of binoculars and speaks aside to his seafaring host. "I can't see a thing through this weather."

"It is early yet. The fog is good to conceal our arrival. Once the sun rises above the horizon, it will burn off quickly." The hosting Cuban remains stationary, with his feet shoulder-width apart and has both hands clenched behind his back. "When we have the first visual contact with Longley's ship, we will need to act quickly."

Jon tries to peer through the murkiness, as the yacht steadily cruises out to the ocean waters beyond. He holds the set of binoculars at his chest and glances to the poised Cuban. "Your friends really want this Captain pretty bad, huh?" Carlos remains rigid and refolds his hands behind his back. He stares out into the shrouding clouds of vapor, as if his gaze could pierce through it. "My associates in Cuba have a long and troubled history with Captain Longley."

"You know him personally?"

"There was a time, long ago, when I thought I did." Carlos pauses and finally clears his throat with a cough. "When you brought me that military-grade life vest, I realized it could only belong to a select few of my former comrades." Jon raises, then, frustrated, lowers the useless distance glasses and wipes the salty moisture from under his eyes. The two stand at the rail of the upper deck as the powerful marine engines reverberate underneath, and the cruising vessel rises and lowers, riding the swells.

Carlos casts a keen eye toward Jon and continues. "Bulletproof life vests are not standard issue in any military. That particular one is lined with a Soviet Kevlar material around the areas of vital organs." The Cuban businessman pauses and lets his words weigh on his apprehensive guest. "When the vest was presented to me, I had hoped that he might have been exterminated. Alas, it appears not to be so."

Jon holds the binoculars up again and squints into the surrounding fog. "He's definitely alive despite being injured. At least, he was still kicking around yesterday."

"Captain Longley and his crew of buccaneers have not been active in these waters for quite some time. I believe it is

your friend, Mister Fulton, who has lured him back again."
The Cuban looks out to the slowly lifting fog-bank hanging
over the ocean and continues. "He is a very intelligent and
military-trained leader, but has been, as the saying goes,
'captain of his own ship' for far, far too long." Carlos takes in
a long, extended breath and lets it out with a melancholy sigh.
"Our seafaring captain has overstepped his intended role, as
well as his economic usefulness, with my Cuban associates."

Jon and Carlos stand quietly alongside one another at
the upper ship rail. The warming breeze of a new day sweeps
over them in the lifting haze and light of morning.

~*~

The surrounding ocean of Gulf waters seem to separate from
the lifting bank of dense fog. The outline of the pirate yacht
waits anchored like a shrouded specter lurking in the mist.
From the uninhabited island, the morning calls of seabirds
chatter and sound out in the dim morning light.

Inside the radio control room, Fulton points the barrel
of his pistol at the radioman and directs him over to where the
other pirate crewman stands near the closed hatch doorway.
The radio operator casually glances at a control near the
intercom, and Fulton calmly offers the two a firm warning.
"Don't you touch anything, and I might not have to use this.
Step over there by the door and be quiet."

The radioman exchanges a guarded look with the other
pirate seaman and obliges the gun wielding, former captive.
Fulton moves to the radio control-panel and changes the
frequency knobs while keeping one eye on the two hostages.
He speaks into the radio receiver and broadcasts over the
selected channel: "Fighting Lady to Key West Air Charters ...
south by east of Dry Tortugas, off Half Moon Key, repeat ...
Fighting Lady to K-W-A-C, south by east of Dry Tortugas..."

The hatch door to the radio room opens and another pirate crew member stares at Fulton, completely astounded. The seaman exchanges a fleeting glance with the other crew in the chamber, and Fulton steps back from the radio controls. Smiling innocently, Fulton keeps the pistol raised at them. "Doesn't any of your ship's crew sleep?"

The crewman in the doorway shifts to make a grab at his sidearm, and Fulton quickly fires his pistol while simultaneously lunging forward toward the open hatch. He pushes past the grasping reach of the radioman and other crew member, as he leaps over the injured pirate at the door and darts into the empty ship corridor. Several following gunshots ricochet through the companionway as Fulton makes his way to the deck above.

The gradually lifting blanket of fog continues to surround the anchored pirate vessel. On the shrouded deck of the ship, a flash of light illuminates the fog-bank and is quickly followed by the *crack* of a gunshot. In quick succession, the hazy mist lights up several more times with a series of blazing reports.

A distinctive, plopping splash off the starboard bow puts an end to the barrage of gunfire, and a silence ensues. From the water, there are sounds of a body surfacing in the waves and the faint splish-splash of swimming. The sounds of paddling strokes are followed by another scattered burst of gunfire that glows the foggy mist with a strobing surge of flashing light.

XXVI

The GPS in Jon's front pants pocket begins to pulse and vibrate with a received message. He takes out the transponder, looks at the set of coordinates on the lit screen and hands it over to the Cuban. "How do your political associates plan to deal with this Captain Longley character once they catch him?" Jon holds the binoculars across his chest and gazes out to the clearing skies, as he stands waiting for Carlos to respond to the message from the pirates.

The Cuban slides the electronic device into his suit jacket pocket and takes a deep, meditative breath. "When we had the support of the Russians, our military was strong and his use of the island for illicit activities was discreet. Unfortunately, times have changed, and Captain Longley's truculent escapades must come to an end."

Eric H. Heisner

There is another pulsing sound from the electronic device, and Carlos draws it from his pocket to read the completed coordinates on the screen. Jon leans over to peer at the message. "Did they send instructions for the exchange?"

Carlos nods with affirmation and tucks the device back into the pocket of his suit jacket. The two stand at the ship rail, as the Cuban yacht cruises through the thinning mist of fog. Jon eyes the seemingly calm Cuban with growing suspicion. "Just remember that nothing can happen until we have Scott safe and free from those pirates."

"Yes, but of course." Carlos forces a consoling grin, turns away and moves inside to initiate their charted course. Left alone on deck, Jon listens to the rumble of engines and lapping of waves alongside. He stares out into the veiled distance and feels a cold chill, despite the steadily warming temperatures.

~*~

The early light of morning is still obscured by a thick haze, as the ascending sun rises over the island of Key West. Rollie stands at the side entry to the Conch Republic Tavern and gives the upstairs buzzer a ring. He peeks in the window to the dark barroom and tries to make out any movement from inside. The door intercom crackles to life, and a sleepy voice emits from the old, dusty speaker. "Hello?"

"Hey, Angie. It's Rollie. Do you know where that new-in-town fella, Springer, is? Something came up about Fulton and I need to find him." The intercom emits static a moment, then fizzles with the sound of her voice. "I'll be right down."

A lone light fixture clicks on, illuminating the middle of the tavern, and the feminine shape of Angie pads barefoot through the shadowy darkness. She steps to the door with only a silk wrap draped loosely, concealing her nakedness.

Island Stepping with Hemingway

She unlocks the door and holds the covering robe in place, while Rollie is captivated by her early morning beauty.

The tavern door cracks open slowly and Angie peeks her head out to converse with the visitor. "It is pretty dammed early... What is it Rollie?"

"Do you have anything on under there?"

"Under where?"

Rollie grins amused as Angie rolls her eyes and frowns at the juvenile joke. "Is that what you came here to wake me up for this early in the morning? I could still be sleeping."

The pilot suddenly turns serious. He tries to avoid gawking at her scantily clad form as she attempts to fix her mussed hair and some of the concealing silk robe falls away. "Uh, I... Ace received a radio message this morning with some coordinates. He was asleep, and it was cut short, but we think it was from Fulton."

"Why are you telling me this?"

Baffled, Rollie stares at her, and then turns to look to the street at his old truck. "I didn't know who else to tell."

"What about that Springer guy, or even the police?"

Rollie shifts his attention to her as he tries to focus. "Every time I stop at his apartment, he isn't anywhere around. Have you seen him?" Rollie jokingly gives a peek around her modestly clad figure to the bar inside.

Unamused, Angie drops her jaw and adjusts her covering wrap. "How old are you now, fifteen?"

"Mentally or physically?"

Angie sighs drowsily and flashes a sympathetic smile. "You'll never change, Rollie. Still likes to fight with the boys and growing older won't make you grow up."

"Hopefully not."

Eric H. Heisner

Pulling her bed-tangled hair back from her neckline, Angie heaves a breath and looks out to Rollie's parked truck. "I haven't seen him since last night."

"When was that?"

Angie frowns at the memory of the encounter with her Cuban admirer. "He was here, having a drink with Carlos."

Rollie seems surprised. "He was? Really? They say anything about going anywhere or where he would be?"

"You know the way Carlos is. That sneaky bastard always looks like he's up to something."

Rollie nods his agreement and moves toward the street. "Thanks, I'll check the docks."

Angie reaches out and grabs his arm, pulling him back. "Hold on, I'm going with you."

Rollie shakes his head "That's really not a good idea."

Angie shoots him a harsh and disapproving expression. "And don't you give me that, *it's not safe for women,* bullshit. I'll grab some clothes and be right down." Releasing his arm, Angie moves back into the dimly lit tavern, then turns and jabs a pointed finger at Rollie. "If you don't stay and wait for me, I'll cancel your bar tab and banish you forever."

Beaten, he shakes his head, and hurriedly waves her on. "Go. Go on... Hurry it up."

In her bare feet, the saloon owner turns away, trots across the tavern floor and quickly ascends the back staircase. Her covering wrap flutters askew of her naked bottom as she disappears from sight, while Rollie stands waiting at the door. He peers out to the misty fog hanging in the street and grunts, "Can't fly till this soup burns off anyway."

XXVII

In the ocean waters past the island keys, the early morning haze remains heavy, lessening with the increasing heat of day. At the bow of the Cuban yacht, Carlos stands alongside Jon as the vessel slows and settles in the gently rolling ocean waves. Jon looks over at his Cuban host questioningly. "Is this it?"

Staring intensely out into the opaque watery surroundings, Carlos nods. "Sí, the coordinates as instructed."

The two stand silently watching toward the horizon and Jon glances down at the money-loaded duffle bag at his feet. The boat rocks on the undulating sea and gentle splashes lap against the idle boat's hull. The overwhelming impression of being at a definite disadvantage, and the impending sensation of claustrophobia, comes over Jon, as he looks out to the gray foggy nothingness all around.

~*~

The Historic Key West Marina is mostly quiet as boat captains prep their rigs for the morning catch of tourist anglers and wait for the fog to burn off. Rollie drives his truck up and parks next to the vintage Cadillac owned by Carlos. He steps out to see the empty boat-slip that typically secures the Cuban yacht and glances over at Angie, as she creaks open the passenger-side truck door. "Watch your door on the caddie. Jorgé knows too well the color of paint on my truck."

Angie looks down at the chipped and rusted truck body with a smirk. "What paint?"

They step around the Cadillac to the yacht berth and, disconcerted, Rollie shakes his head. "Damn, why didn't he tell me?" Rollie turns to Angie with a melancholy expression. "I should have warned him to be more wary and not so trusting of Carlos and his absurd schemes."

Angie grimaces as she squints through the morning haze, past the moored sailboats, to the open waters of the ocean beyond. "I think he understood, but felt out of options."

"What could make him think Carlos was an option?"

A dusky, concealed figure peeks out from behind the tackle-supply shack on the wharf and gives a shrill whistle. The two visitors turn to the sound, as the striking, bearded figure of Aston appears through the hazy fog. The island native strolls casually toward the onlookers, as he tosses his long hair back from his face and tilts his head knowingly. "Yous done missed them by more'n an hour." Angie and Rollie look to the local island sage with the colorful parrot, head-tucked and seemingly asleep, rested on his shoulder. "Eh, Rollie mon, you recover much from that knockdown?"

Rollie grins and traces the faded, yellowish bruise on his face. "Show me a few more techniques, and we'll get 'em next time we're in the ring."

Island Stepping with Hemingway

Angie moves past Rollie and steps closer to question Aston. "Did you happen to see Carlos' boat leave?"

Aston seems to be hiding something behind his back, as he nods his head to the nearby tide wall. "Was fishing early just o'er beyond, when theys pulled out 'fore daybreak."

Lapping waves in the marina and the dull clunking of boat hulls smacking the wood pier continue, as Rollie walks over to stand alongside Angie. He nods to Aston and inquires, "Was that new guy to the island with him?"

Aston grins and, by the scruff of the neck, pulls Casey Kettles out from behind. "Cain't say I know, but he might."

Casey frowns at his vagabond captor, then feigns a smile to the seaplane pilot. "Hello, Rollie old boy…"

Somewhat surprised, Rollie turns his attention from the street-kid to the native islander. "What was he doing here?"

"I gots here jest as they was untying 'n he was already 'round 'bouts, creeping 'round like a bottom-feeder catfish."

The teenager starts to squirm under Aston's hawk-like grasp, until Angie squats down to speak diplomatically with the youth. "Are you alright, Casey?"

The boy smiles genially at the female and rolls his eyes up to Aston, who retains a firm grip on Casey's shirt collar. "I'm just doin' dandy. Don't I look it?"

Rollie nods approval to Aston and leans toward Casey. "Always into it, huh kid? Did you see where they went?"

Casey smirks at the pilot and tries to act smart. "They was in a boat, so I guess they was headed out to sea."

"Which direction?"

Casey hangs in Aston's grip and gets out his glasses. "Headed west 'round the island, I suppose."

"Who was aboard?" Rollie meets the boy's obstinate stare and notices him cast a quick wink to Angie. The pilot gives a signal to Aston and the islander gives the boy a shake, cuffing him lightly behind the ear. Casey peers up at Aston and the parrot and then to Rollie, as he groans and speaks up. "The mainlander was aboard with Carlos and his sea-ape."

Attempting to put on some parental sternness, Rollie frowns at the teenage vagrant. "Is there anything else you need to tell us, Casey?"

Wearing his yellow-rimmed sunglasses in spite of the foggy surroundings, Casey gazes over at Aston, still holding him by the shirt collar. "You're wrinkling my shirt, bro."

Angie leans forward to Casey and touches his cheek. "You should be home in bed, not running around out here." She gives a commanding look to Aston, who grins innocently and then releases his grip on the teenager.

Reaching out, Aston thumps Casey hard over the head, pushing the boy's neck down into his shoulders like a turtle. "Yes lit'le boy, ya should be home in bed with dreams of pilfering bulging pockets." Angie gives Aston another stern gaze, and the island sage casually strokes the bird on his shoulder. "Dat is what dis boy would dream 'bout." He looks down at the boy and grins.

Casey adjusts his shirt collar, pulling his shoulders back defiantly. "I sure don't like the nasty dreams that come from the grunts of old, sweaty bums humping in the night." The three grownups regard the derelict teenager with genuine compassion, at a loss for the right words. Casey puts on a snide face, resenting their obvious sympathy to his brothel-upbringing, and sneers. "It's just a dumb joke, you bunch of squares. Are we through here?" With an offhand gesture, Rollie confirms Casey's dismissal.

Waving a flick of his skinny wrist, Casey steps around the small group. His hand motion looks mockingly familiar to Carlos' goodbye salute, with the exception of a middle finger jutting skyward. "See ya losers! Wouldn't want to be ya!"

Island Stepping with Hemingway

They watch, as the juvenile delinquent trots away and disappears amongst the mist-shrouded boats in the marina.

Rollie walks to his pickup truck and turns back to the man with the sleeping parrot tucked on his shoulder. "Aston, stop by the hanger sometime later in the week. I have some more of those barrels you can use."

A wide-beaming smile spreads across the native islander's features. He bobs his head agreeably, and the snoozing parrot seems to wake for a moment to mimic the action. "Yes, sir. Thanks much, Rollie. I was wanting to build an addition to my floating palace." The islander steps back into the foggy shroud then hunkers down and performs several shadowboxing moves. "If you want to keep your head attached in the ring, perhaps I will teach you some of the secrets my Grandpapa taught Hemingway." Rollie gives Aston a thumbs-up, as the enigmatic figure fades into the veiling mist.

Angie stares off to where Casey departed and then focuses on the empty yacht slip. "Do you think that Springer fella is in some trouble because of what Scott was into?"

Rollie pulls open the creaking door of the truck and meets her troubled gaze. "I don't think he even realizes how serious a situation he might be in."

"Smugglers?"

"If Carlos is involved, it could be worse yet."

"You think we should contact the police now?"

Standing behind the truck door, Rollie scans his gaze into the fog-clouded marina. "I'm not sure if telling the cops about the little we do know, involving a friend of Fulton's, will help the situation any."

Angie appears pensive, as she slides past the parked Cadillac and opens the passenger-side door of the truck. She eases inside onto the fabric-covered, squeaky springs of the vehicle's bench seat and replies, "The problem with Scott is you either love him or hate him."

The repetitive clanging thump of tethered boats and ship-rigging in the marina continues, as the late morning mist still clings low along the coastal waterline. The pickup truck starts up with a rumbling growl and grindingly shifts into gear. A small, adolescent head, wearing a pair of yellow-rimmed sunglasses, peeks out from a concealing structure on the pier. He watches the old truck turn on its high beams, reverse back a few feet and then roll forward into the haze.

XXVIII

Over the expanse of ocean waters, the clinging layer of fog begins to burn off, as the sun crests higher over the horizon. With the engines rumbling at a low idle, the Cuban luxury yacht gently rises and falls on the surface of the deep waters that surround them. Everything seems calm with the exception of soft-lapping waves smacking against the hull of the waiting maritime vessel.

The eerie haze continues to diffuse until, suddenly, the pirate ship, with its menacing panel of tinted windows, materializes through the vapor. From the deck of their yacht, Jon and Carlos watch anxiously as the sleek pirate vessel moves steadily nearer. They both stare silently, in nervous admiration, until Jon turns to Carlos and softly whispers, "He's watching from behind those dark windows."

Carlos gawks ahead at the approaching pirate vessel. As if in a daydream, he stands at the ship rail, unmoved.

Beginning to question their hurriedly-formed rescue strategy, Jon peers over at the non-reaction of his host. "Hey Carlos... Are you alright?"

The Cuban businessman finally takes a deep, reassuring breath and bends his head slightly. "It appears Captain Longley has done quite well for himself. He has a much superior and updated watercraft than he did many years ago."

With the Cuban's startling lack of assurance, Jon starts to feel unsettled. "Is that gonna be a problem?"

Carlos half-heartedly glances at Jon, beside him at the rail. "Señor Springer, this was not what I was anticipating."

With the binoculars raised to his face, Jon anxiously observes the oncoming pirate ship, as the resonating quiet around them intensifies the pulsing beat of the heart pounding in his chest. He lowers the glasses from his sightline and turns to Carlos "What the hell! You're kidding, right?"

The Cuban gulps audibly, and his hands quiver on the rail. "That is a much larger, and very well equipped, vessel."

"Yes! I was on it the other day! I told you that!"

"It is just more than I expected."

"How much more than expected?"

"I am just a businessman, not a hardened mercenary."

"What were you planning and not telling me, Carlos?"

The Cuban apprehensively looks over his shoulder to where his manservant, stands at the yacht's power controls. Jorgé shrugs his wide, hunched shoulders, and the henchman's gaze moves from his boss to the approaching pirate vessel. Carlos turns back to his guest, flicks his tongue out to moisten his pursed lips and forces a confident outward facade for Jon. "All will be well. We will deal with the situation as planned."

Island Stepping with Hemingway

Short of much reassurance from his maritime host, Jon looks at Carlos skeptically. His palms clammy with sweat, he nervously removes the binocular strap from around his neck. They both watch as the lustrous pirate vessel slowly slices through the rolling waters as it cruises closer.

~*~

Stock Island is situated along the main highway bridge on the opposite side of the island of Key West from Old Town. The dilapidated waterfront docks and shipyards are filled with shrimpers and lobstermen who were pushed off the bigger island when the tourist and cruise-ship trade took over. Now the home base of a working-class crowd, the lesser island has the cast-off attitude and laid-back personality that was once the identity of the entire chain of Keys.

Anchored not too far offshore, in a rent-free patch of water and partially sheltered by thick mangroves, floats a makeshift collection of lashed-together barrels. Perched atop the mishmash deck is an elaborate sea shanty which appears to be something taken right from the tale of Tom Sawyer or the Kon-Tiki. The assembled floating abode is creative haven and private residence to a particular parrot-toting, free-wheeling, island sage.

The rattle and clank of the overly garish-decorated bicycle is heard, as the early morning fog slowly disperses. Long tangles of matted hair flow back from under his head scarf, as Aston careens the festooned contraption toward a stand of palm trees and dismounts while skidding sidelong to a stop. The devoted parrot flaps its wings and clings to its owner's shoulder, as Aston leans the bike over on a cut-off tree stump. Stepping his sandaled feet down into the root-tangled water, he wades thigh deep to find a dinghy hidden in the dense watergrass.

Seated in the small boat, wet from the middle down, Aston rows out toward his barrel-buoyed homemade fortress. He grips a homemade paddling contraption consisting of an old broomstick handle lashed to the end of a bent street sign. He dips the oddly constructed paddle into the water and pulls, with long, lazy strokes, toward the anchored raft.

On the salty breeze, the familiar noise of whirling propellers catches his attention, and he pauses in his efforts. The air-chopping sounds originate from across the channel in the direction of the airport, and Aston can faintly make out the colors of the Coast Guard helicopter lifting off. The morning sun begins to break through the early fog, burning off the cloudy haze and creating patches of clear, blue sky. With the homemade paddle across his lap, Aston stares into the shrouded heavens until the sounds of the government chopper fade.

XXIX

A wide patch of clearing sky finally spreads open at the watery meeting spot of the two water-crafts. Jon and Carlos stand at the starboard rail watching as the pirate vessel moves closer, and the swinging metal clank of an opening hatch is heard. With astonishing speed, the pirate crew swarms out to form-up along the deck, with military assault rifles in hand.

The two oceangoing yachts come within a few yards of each other, and Captain Longley steps up to the port-side bow. The first mate, Jacek, appears beside him. Peering down at the expectant twosome on the Cuban yacht, the pirate captain maintains a dour demeanor as he speaks. "Well, hello Carlos... It's been a very long time, has it not? Are you still attempting to save face, and nurture those seeds of political intrigue, by hiding out in the Keys?"

Jon looks aside, concerned about his quiet Cuban host. After a long, uncomfortable moment of silence Jon calls over to the larger vessel. "Where's Fulton?"

Captain Longley leans forward, puts his hands to the port rail and stares down. "A man who gets to the business at hand, I like that. No time for chit chat. Where is the ransom?"

The money-loaded duffle rests at Jon's feet, behind the curtained ship rail, and Jon hesitantly glances down at it. Thoughts of his entire savings stuffed into a canvas tote race through his mind. Finally, he reaches down, lifts the duffle from the deck and holds it at his side. Jon peers up at Longley. "I have it here."

Captain Longley scrutinizes the dimensions of the duffle bag carefully from a distance and nods his approval. He gestures to his first mate with a raised hand and wags two fingers forward. "Have them bring out our honored guest." The strained encounter is stagnant until a single, black-hooded figure is brought out and positioned at the ship rail beside Captain Longley.

Jon stares up to the pirates and the unidentifiable person under the concealing cloth sack. "I need to see him before I surrender the ransom."

Jacek responds by tossing a coiled length of marine line across to Carlos' yacht deck. Jon looks down at the curled rope as the end of the tether lands in an oddly familiar shape of a hangman's noose. He turns his nervous gaze back up to the pirate captain and calls out, "No ransom until I see him."

Captain Longley continues to lean on the ship rail and replies, "Tie on the money, and we'll send him right over."

Reluctantly kneeling down, Jon threads a double loop of rope through the duffle bag handles. He looks up at Jacek, holding the line at the other end of the exchange and rises.

Island Stepping with Hemingway

Placing his foot on the bag, Jon waits to identify the captive. "Let me see that he's okay. Then, you'll get the ransom."

In the distance, over the rising and falling ocean skyline, the *thump, thump, thump* of a chopper's rotary blades can be heard steadily approaching the location of the exchange. Captain Longley perks his ear to the light wind and scowls. "What the hell is this?"

Just as surprised, Jon turns to Carlos and, in exasperation, asks, "Is this a part of the plan?"

In an instant, Jon is almost knocked off his feet as the duffle bag is jerked away and over the side-rail of the yacht. Jon lunges, too late, for the money-filled duffle, as it swings away and bounces twice on the port hull of the pirate yacht. On the third rebound, the loose rope slips through the duffle handles and the bag of ransom drops to the water below.

Jon, Carlos and Captain Longley simultaneously lean forward to gape over the railing at the loaded bag of cash, bobbing gently on the sloshing waves between the boats. They all turn their attention skyward, as the oncoming helicopter, clearly identified with the colorful orange markings of the United States Coast Guard, flies nearer. The pirate captain quickly assesses the fouled exchange and contemplates the imminent arrival of the military helicopter. He glares down at Jon and barks, "Did I not forewarn you of dire consequences, Mister Springs! You want him now?"

Longley draws a pistol from the underarm holster on his military vest and holds it out toward the hooded hostage. With the gun barrel pressed to the man's shrouded head, the pirate captain stands firm as Jon pleads, "No ... Don't do it!" Everyone flinches, as the *flashing snap* of a gunshot registers and the hostage in the dark hood slumps to the ship's railing. Jacek gives the executed body a shove and the limp form flops overboard into the water, near the floating ransom.

A sickened sensation sweeps over Jon, as he stares dumbfounded at the hooded, gunshot body slowly sinking beneath the clear ocean waves. In the curving, black reflection off the gleaming wet hull of the pirate vessel, Jon notices a solitary figure appear on the upper deck of the Cuban yacht. He turns to see Jorgé take position with a tubular rocket-grenade-launcher perched on his broad shoulder. He feels Carlos' grip on his arm and is fiercely tugged to the boat deck, as the Cuban henchman ignites the explosive missile with a loud hissing blast.

The rocket grenade detonates on the forecastle of the pirate yacht, rocking it in the water with its fiery concussion. The unexpected detonation sends pirate crewmen careening away from the explosion, as others rush along the deck, automatic weapons at the ready. Carlos shoves Jon ahead of him, as he scurries for cover below deck. "Hurry, go below!" As Jon tumbles down the short stairway to the lower cabin, Carlos yells to the henchman with the expended launcher. "Jorgé, get us out of here! Quick!"

XXX

The foredeck of the pirate vessel smolders with the resulting blast of the rocket-propelled grenade. Several crewmen scramble to extinguish destructive flames, as others unleash rounds of machine-gun fire at the opposing yacht. Like a beacon of defeat, a thick plume of black smoke swirls skyward from the ship, beckoning the U.S. Coast Guard helicopter.

In a hail of gunfire, Carlos follows Jon below deck as the marine engines roar to full throttle. Slowly pulling away from the pirate ship, Carlos's yacht takes several barrages of machine-gun fire, until it finally moves out of rifle range. Inside the yacht's lower cabin, the two listen as the plinking of bullet-lead across the stern finally ceases.

His ears ringing from the recent explosion, Jon squats with his face cradled in his hands. He finally looks up at Carlos and mutters, "We killed him."

Carlos paces the yacht's lower cabin area and gazes through the bullet-spattered windows to the burning pirate vessel in the near-distance. "That wasn't Mister Fulton."

"How do you know that?"

The Cuban takes a fat rolled cigar from his inner jacket pocket and attempts to light the tip with trembling hands. "That's the oldest trick in the book."

"What kind of books are *you* reading?"

"Hostage exchange one-o'-one. Did you see the way the hooded man was dressed? Mister Scott Fulton surely outfits more like Errol Flynn than Nick Nolte."

In dazed bewilderment, Jon stares at Carlos, as the Cuban finally lights the big cigar between his white teeth and puffs out a halo of smoke. "You think he's not dead based on what he was wearing?"

Carlos moves across the cabin to the unharmed wet bar setup and begins to mix drinks to calm their unsettled nerves. "In all likelihood he was killed already, before the exchange, but that's not your fault."

The realization of the grim truth of the situation begins to sink in for Jon. "What about the coast guard helicopter?"

"The U.S. Coast Guard is quite capable of handling pirates like our friendly captain of the high seas. We will find out what happened... when we get to Cuba." The Cuban businessman stirs two cocktails, sets one aside for Jon, and takes a long, gulping swallow from his own.

Jon redirects his gaze from the floor over to Carlos tending bar and stares in disbelief. "Cuba? I can't go to Cuba."

Carlos dutifully acknowledges Jon with his raised cocktail glass and finishes off the remainder of his freshly-made drink. "I cannot go back to United States with a bullet-riddled boat and avoid uncomfortable questioning."

Island Stepping with Hemingway

"Wouldn't it be considered illegal for me to just show up in Cuba without a passport or papers?"

"Yes."

Jon seems rightly baffled by the Cuban's casual tone. "Yes? What do you mean, *yes*? I will probably be arrested and thrown in jail as soon as we hit Cuban waters." Eyeing Jon's untouched cocktail, Carlos prepares another, stronger, drink for himself and offers a feeble shrug. "We are most likely in Cuban waters now."

The swiftly cruising watercraft seems to choke, falter and slow; causing Jon and Carlos to exchange a worried look. The acrid smell of something burning tickles their nostrils. Simultaneously, both men hold their breath, as the boat's rumbling engines audibly sputter, clank and cease running. The gunfire-damaged yacht sways with the ocean swells, continues its forward momentum and drifts along quietly. Carlos moves to a control panel, switches on the yacht's intercom and hesitantly inquires, "Jorgé, what's happened?"

From above-deck at the stern, the foul, smoky odor of burnt oil floods the room. Carlos drops his drink glass in the sink and hustles upstairs from the lower cabin. Jon follows closely, and they witness Jorgé using a small fire extinguisher on the whipping fingers of flame coming from the bullet-damaged engine box. Carlos gazes nervously out to the distant skyline and gasps, "What is going on, Jorgé? We can't be stopping out here!"

The henchman continues to douse the persistent conflagration with clouds of white spray and, with a startlingly alarmed expression for a big man, glimpses at Carlos in panic. "The gunshots damaged the engines."

Carlos gapes at the clear sky on the horizon, then to Jon a quick moment and finally at Jorgé. "We cannot stay here. Patch it best you can. We must keep moving on our course."

With the engine-compartment fire finally put out, Jorgé nods obediently and begins to sweep away the extinguisher foam. Carlos keeps a vigilant eye on the surrounding waters and reaches over to pat Jon reassuringly on his near shoulder. "Keep a watchful lookout for any large boats or airplanes, especially those of the Cuban military."

Jon gazes out to the bright blue ocean all around them. "Will we need to flag them down?"

"No, that would be very, very bad."

"What if they were to help us?"

"It would most likely be just the opposite."

Jon notices Carlos pacing the yacht's deck and notices his host's restlessness increase with each passing moment. "What about your Cuban associates we planned to meet?" Carlos pivots on a heel and waggles his head despondently. "They are not with the military and cannot aid us on this." The nervous Cuban climbs the stairway to the upper sundeck, hoping to improve his vantage position. Jon stands at the lower side-rail of the yacht and, in frustration, calls up to Carlos, "What kind of connections *do* you actually have?"

"Faith, Señor Springer… You must have faith."

Without receiving the faintest hint of reassurance, Jon looks out over the vast ocean and heaves a sigh of disgust.

XXXI

At the Coast Guard headquarters on Trumbo Point, all seems peaceful and quiet as Rollie's truck drives past the closed gate. The truck rolls to a squeaking stop and sits idling, with a clear view through a chain link fence to the airfield and shipyard.

Both hands gripping the wheel, Rollie pensively gazes over at Angie beside him. She senses the morose change in his mood and looks out past the razor-wire-topped security fence to the shipyard beyond. "Is something wrong?"

"The rescue chopper is gone."

"So, what does that mean?"

Rollie looks at the patrol boats remaining in the slips and mumbles aloud, "Looks like the big Cutter is out too." Angie waits patiently for Rollie to clue her in on his thoughts. Instead, he cranks the big steering wheel and does a U-turn in the street. He hammers on the gas pedal, barks the rear tires and drives toward his home base of operations.

The metal truck cab rattles, as Angie holds onto the door handle and looks to Rollie inquiringly. "What else did you see out there, Rollie?"

He chews his lip while breathing through his nostrils. "Something is going on out there, and the boys in the Coast Guard are already onto it. We need to get back and be ready to be in the air as soon as the visibility clears."

Rollie drives quickly as Angie braces herself on the squeaky bench seat, feeling the reverberation of the old pickup truck around her. She stares ahead as they travel across the island. "Never a dull moment around here..."

~*~

In the open waters, the bullet-damaged Cuban yacht continues to sway, powerless in the ocean waves. Jon climbs the stairs to the upper observation deck as one of the dual boat engines finally begins to crank and turn over. Carlos stands with a set of binoculars at his chest and surveys the seascape. He looks over at Jon, raises the glasses to his face and scans the view. "See, my friend, no problem."

A single yacht engine rumbles, and the damaged watercraft begins to slowly chug forward. A sense of relief fills the air, as a watery wake develops behind them. Alongside Carlos, Jon holds the rail of the upper deck as the yacht bounces through the waves. "Do you see anything?"

"Nothing yet..." Carlos lowers the binoculars and puts his finger on the intercom button on the panel at his side. "Jorgé, set course for Havana. Ready the inflatable launch." Jon takes a breath, then turns to Carlos to inquire the obvious. "Do I need to know...? What's the launch for?"

"You said you would not like to accompany us on our necessary visit to Cuban shores. We have an inflatable raft down below, so that is the alternative."

Island Stepping with Hemingway

"Your great plan is to leave me in the middle of the ocean in a rubber dinghy?"

"It is not essentially the middle of the ocean."

Jon looks out to the rolling waves "It's near enough!"

Carlos flashes his trademark smile. "Cuban refugees do it all the time with much, much less."

Jon develops a sickly pallor as he stares out at the endless expanse of water. "I don't think I want to paddle my way back to Key West. There might be more than a few questions about how I happened to get out here."

Attempting to conceal his apprehension, Carlos forces an uneasy chuckle and tries to maintain his reassuring smile. "We radioed your friend for a special rescue engagement."

"Who? The Key West police detective?"

"No, the other one... The cowboy with the seaplane..."

"To pick me up in Cuban waters?"

Carlos seems nonchalant and puts the binoculars to his face again. "He knows his way around the area quite well." Jon stares out to the undulating ocean waters. The reality of his impending predicament twists his stomach into an uncomfortable knot.

~*~

Aboard the cruising Cuban yacht, the distinct quiet drone of airplane engines can be heard in the far distance. The bullet-damaged vessel continues to charge through the rolling whitecaps, as Jorgé unrolls a rope ladder over the side and readies the inflatable launch. He dumps the un-inflated rubber raft over the rear of the boat and ties the lead line to a docking cleat below the rail on the stern.

On the upper deck, Carlos puts the set of binoculars to his face and scans the skies for the intercepting seaplane. The faint outline of the high-winged, Grumman flying boat can be seen in the distant sky. Carlos lowers the focused eyepieces and smiles widely "Mister Springer, your salvation comes from on high!"

Moving from his position, looking past the stern, where the rubber lifeboat is being launched, Jon steps toward Carlos. "Yeah, just in time." All three of them on the yacht watch as the amphibious aircraft soars nearer, wings low, nearly skimming the ocean waves. The seaplane roars past them and banks along the skyline for a landing approach.

Something else appears faintly on the horizon and Carlos suddenly raises the pair of binoculars to his face again. He twists the focus knob on the eyepieces and can't seem to believe what he is seeing. "This cannot be...! Impossible!" Lowering the binoculars, Carlos removes the strap from around his neck and tosses them aside. He turns Jon away and quickly ushers his guest toward the rear stairway that descends to the main ship deck. "Got to go! You must hurry into the lifeboat."

Jon watches as the Key West Air Charter seaplane touches down and skims lightly across the choppy waves. Nearing the stairs, Jon turns, resisting Carlos' urging. "They'll be a few minutes yet before they arrive. What's your hurry?"

The anxious Cuban grabs Jon firmly by the arm, directs him to the descending stairway and all but shoves him downward. "We cannot wait for the joyous reunion of your deliverance. Jorgé and I must be going on our way."

At the bottom of the stairway, Carlos addresses his maritime henchman, pointing him inside to the ship wheel. There is urgency to his voice, as he barks the commands with a harsh Spanish accent. "Jorgé, take the helm and get us on direct course for Havana! There is no time for dilly-dallies." Jon is unceremoniously pushed to the stern railing and promptly directed over the side into the waiting dinghy.

Island Stepping with Hemingway

Watching the now-inflated yellow life raft drifting nimbly in the yacht's churned wake, Jon gets an uneasy, sick sensation. He hesitates at the idea of being dumped in the ocean... even for a short time. Jon notices the Cuban's odd behavior and lingers as he eases over the side of the yacht. "What is going on, Carlos?"

The Cuban helps Jon at the top of the uncoiled rope ladder and takes a fleeting look to the other side of the yacht. He waves goodbye and puts on a show with his phony grin. "Time for us to be leaving, Señor Springer. Have a nice trip!" As soon as Jon's foot reaches the dinghy, Carlos begins to pull the ladder up the side.

Close behind, trailing in the luxury yacht's single engine wake, the rubber life boat steadily follows along. Carlos hoists the last dangling rung of rope ladder to the rear deck of the yacht and gives Jon a brisk farewell gesture. Standing alone in the small inflatable life raft, Jon watches in bewilderment as the Cuban quickly unties the tethered line.

"Carlos, why the hasty sendoff?"

The grinning expression of the seafaring host quickly fades, and Carlos ducks away while his yelling voice can still be heard from over the side. "Jorgé, go! Full engines ahead!" The sole engine rumbles with increasing throttle and a surge of churned ocean gurgles up from the underwater propeller. In a moment, the accelerating yacht pushes forward, abandoning the inflatable life boat in its v-shaped wake. Carlos reappears at the stern, and, in his cavalier way, salutes Jon. "So long! Hope to see you again someday in Key West."

Jon sits down in the bottom of the small rubber raft, as it bobbles in the remaining wake. He watches Carlos withdraw inside as the bullet and smoke-damaged yacht motors away. Gazing around to locate the seaplane, Jon notices the dark, outline of the approaching pirate ship.

Eric H. Heisner

The rubber raft squeaks as Jon shifts to his knees and looks over the bow. He hauls in the partly submerged length of lead rope and casts a glance to the departing Cuban yacht. Jon slaps the rubber raft and growls, "Damn you, Carlos!"

The thundering blast of a deck cannon booms, followed by another, as guns in the upper hull of the pirate vessel are revealed. The shots are followed by nearby splashes of water, as the gun crews gauge the distance to the bright-yellow target. Riding up the swell of a cresting wave, Jon quickly locates the Grumman flying boat plowing through choppy waters, heading directly toward him.

To the south, the fleeing Cuban yacht continues to travel under full throttle, and Jon shakes his head angrily. "Carlos, you better watch it if I make it back to Key West." Sitting helpless in the rubber dingy, Jon watches as the seaplane steadily moves closer and another volley of high-caliber cannon-fire explodes from the hull of the pirate ship. Jon shifts lower in the inflatable raft, as each blasting round splashes nearer to the mark. "C'mon Rollie! Hurry it up!"

XXXII

Through the water-level seaplane cockpit window, Rollie can be seen nudging the overhead engine throttle levers. He steers through the cresting ocean waves toward the small rubber life boat bobbing between the obstructing barriers of rising swells. The seaplane drifts sideways in the current and Rollie operates the tail rudder, attempting to keep on course.

Rising from her seat in the co-pilot chair, Angie peers over the rolling ocean waves. "He's coming up over there... Don't plow over him with the props."

Rollie looks over at her disparagingly. "This isn't as easy as it looks, and you're not helping things." He reaches overhead and keeps his hand spread between the throttle-adjustment levers, attempting to balance thrust between the pair of engines.

Rollie looks out his port side window and watches the spinning propellers slice through the rising tips of the waves.

"Open water maneuvers are a lot more general than specific. With these conditions, I'm not only dealing with the wind... There's a heavy current pushing us around."

Angie clenches her jaw, nervous, and peers out the window. "This will all be a waste if you chop him into fish bait."

Becoming a bit annoyed, the pilot gives his female copilot a stern look and tilts his head toward the back cargo-area of the winged watercraft. "Why don't you go in the back and be ready to open that hatch when we get close enough." As Angie slides past Rollie, he grumbles, "Be sure to watch out for any rogue waves, so we don't get swamped."

~*~

The life raft rises and falls on ocean waves, rotating directionless, as the high-winged seaplane cruises nearer to it. A wingtip pontoon passes close by as a swelling upsurge of water churns through the whirling propeller, dousing Jon with a spray of water. Jon shakes it off and stoops low in the life raft, as the two floating vessels dip and weave toward each other on the undulating ocean surface.

As they steadily approach, the pirates continue to adjust their aim toward the intended target. With each blast of the cannon, Jon cringes and waits for the resulting splash of water. Another deck gun fires off and, only a few yards away, the projectile slams into the ocean's surface, plunging to the depths with a fizzling trail of tiny bubbles.

The plane's rear-access hatch swings open to the inside, and Jon tosses the coil of rope from the inflatable life raft to the shadowed figure crouched near the doorway. Another booming blast erupts from the pirate ship, and Jon instinctively ducks. He glimpses past the rescuing seaplane rollicking on the choppy surface to the aggressive pirate yacht moving steadily closer. "Hurry, pull me in!"

Island Stepping with Hemingway

The slack of the tow-line gets hauled to the rear hatch as another shot of cannon fire blasts from the pirate ship. The flying projectile skims the surface of the water and sinks dangerously close to the seaplane. Jon watches a rumbling belch of exhaust spew from the dual radial engines as they throttle-up. The tethered lifeline connecting the water-bound seaplane to the inflatable launch becomes taut as the plane surges forward.

Another blast of the pirate cannon hits the wave just below the raised tail-section of the flying boat, rocking it forward in the water. The splash of displaced water sprays over the rubber raft and the rear portion of the aircraft. Jon braces himself low in the life boat as the high-winged engines roar, propelling the seaplane forward and sending a curling wake of water out from the stepped hull.

~*~

The Key West Air Charters seaplane moves at a steady clip through the choppy, open ocean with the tethered life boat bouncing along in its V-shaped wake. Jon presses tight inside the walls of the inflatable raft while skimming the broken waves, trying to keep from capsizing. The rubber boat swings outside the seaplane's churned path, hits a cresting wave and launches high through the propeller-misted air. Jon braces himself snuggly to the bottom of the boat and winces, as the raft gets a jolt from the attached lead line and slams back to the water's surface. "Holy crap!"

Trailing behind the speeding seaplane the rubber raft crests another upsurge and launches skyward. Jon sneaks a glimpse behind, noting the increasing distance from the pursuing pirate yacht, as the lifeboat smashes to the ocean's surface and slides back into the seaplane's wake. He holds tight to the sides of the raft, as the constant spray of water from the forward thrusting propellers wash over him.

The high-throttled roar from the dual engines suddenly decelerates. The seaplane glides forward as it settles lower on its hull. It slows to near an idle, and the inflatable launch is once again pulled toward the side entry hatch at the tail-section. Several more cannon blasts splash into the water, just out of range, as a friendly voice calls to Jon. "Stop playing with your dingy and get inside here, you durned fool."

The rubber boat, with Jon firmly clenched inside, is pulled toward the rear hatch. It comes alongside, and Jon is suddenly face-to-face with the somewhat worse-for-wear, but familiar, features of Scott Fulton. Jon pushes his wet hair aside and wipes the blur of saltwater from his eyes, hardly recognizing his old friend. "Is that you, Scott?"

Fulton lets go of the lead-line and reaches out to Jon. "We'll save all the mushy stuff for later. Get yer ass in here!" Jon takes Scott's hand and climbs inside the rear hatch. As the seaplane moves forward, the coil of wet rope is tossed outside, and the rubber life raft drifts free of the floating hull. The engines on the flying boat promptly roar to full throttle, as a spray of prop-wash surges past the closing hatch.

XXXIII

On the pursuing pirate yacht, from behind the forward panel of tinted windows, Captain Longley observes the sea rescue. He calmly witnesses the Grumman seaplane pick up speed, leaving a trail of ocean spray and the empty life raft behind. The pirate captain crosses his arms over his chest as the flying boat nimbly lifts into the air and skims over the rolling waves into the blue heavens, absconding to the sunlit horizon.

Another blast of cannon artillery discharges from the deck of the pirate ship, arcing across the distance. One of the projectiles splashes into the spot of ocean previously occupied by the seaplane as the other round crashes into the side of the abandoned life raft. The inflatable rubber launch doubles over with the puncturing impact and sinks beneath the surface.

"Cease fire ..."

Captain Longley watches with a cold expression, as the seaplane banks to the north and fades into the clear blue sky.

He looks to a handgun placed on the ship's lit control panel and releases his finger from the intercom button. He unzips his armored life vest and sets the tactical garment over a chair beside the dripping wet duffle bag containing the ransom.

~*~

The twin radial engines on the flying boat roar in sync as the rescuing seaplane flies back to the island of Key West. With a smile, Rollie peeks back from the cockpit into the cargo area to greet his new guest. "Welcome aboard, Springer."

As he mops his hair with a beach towel, Jon offers a grateful salute toward the seaplane pilot. "Thanks for the sea rescue. It was in the nick of time, too. I would have ended up in pirate hands, a watery grave or a Cuban prison!"

"Always glad to be of service." The pilot gestures a thumbs-up and pivots back to the flight controls.

Jon lowers the wet towel to stare mystified at Angie and his ransomed friend. "Hello... What the hell, Scott?"

Fulton shrugs guiltlessly and, with a sly wink, glances at Angie. "I wasn't going to wait for you to break your little piggy bank and come to my rescue."

A hollow sensation of dread comes over Jon as he thinks of his entire savings lost in the ransom payment. He gawps at Fulton, not sure if he wants to hit or hug him. "Damn Scott... I did break the bank to come rescue you!"

Scott chuckles glibly. "Sorry... I was already gone."

Completely stunned, Jon can't stop staring at his friend. "I thought you were dead!"

Angie steps in and takes the beach towel from Jon. "Why would you say such a terrible thing? Didn't you know Scott is like a cat with nine lives?"

Scott smirks as he grasps Angie around the midsection. "I do like to visit with the kitties."

Island Stepping with Hemingway

With an irritated roll of her eyes, she pushes him away. "Sometimes you're just as bad as Carlos. Speaking of the devil, where was he off to?"

Jon leans against the curved wall in his wet clothes and grunts, "Carlos left me stranded and headed for Cuba."

Scott nods. "Sounds like his mode of operation."

White clouds drift through blue skies outside the rounded aircraft windows, as Jon stares, dazed, at his friend. "We saw someone who we thought was you, get executed."

Scott looks to Angie, then back at Jon, and smiles. "Takes more'n a gang of modern-day pirates to kill me off."

Jon continues to be baffled by his longtime friend. He is torn between the intense feelings of dread concerning the complete loss of his accumulated savings and the joyful sight of seeing Scott Fulton alive again. He finally snaps out of it and sinks against the riveted wall in the cargo area of the flying boat. "You really cost me a load of cash, buddy."

"You were actually going to pay that crazy ransom?"

Jon pushes his wet hair aside from his face, looks up at the rescuers and sighs dejected, "Yeah, I was going to pay it."

Scott looks at Angie and then around, curiously. "Where is it?"

Feeling worse by the minute, Jon mumbles, "It was dropped in the ocean, off the back of the Carlos' boat just before the shit hit the fan."

Angie truly appears sympathetic. "The entire ransom?"

Feeling weak at the mere thought of the vast amount, Jon tilts his head back as Angie sits beside him for comfort. He clears his throat and looks up at Scott, then over to Angie. "That canvas duffle contained nearly everything I'm worth."

Angie brushes her fingers through Jon's wet hair as he gazes up at the rows of rivets lining the inside of the seaplane. "You're worth a whole lot more to your friends."

Scott kneels by Jon and pats him kindly on the knee. "You know I'm probably good for it, one way or another."

With a glimmer of hope, Jon groans at his longtime pal, "I would be hurting pretty bad financially if you weren't."

Scott displays a remorseful expression and lowers his voice as he leans in closer. "I don't have any money, per se, right now, but some of my diversified financial investments are bound to pay off in the near future."

Jon looks to his longtime friend and raises his eyebrows in a pleading show of disbelief. With a laughing grin, Scott taps him on the shoulder. "What are you worried about?"

Jon puts his elbows to his knees, appearing as if he is about to break down and cry then murmurs, "I'm broke…"

Fulton teasingly gives Jon a hard nudge with his foot. "It will be back to the old *J.T. Springs* pulp adventure novels for you my friend."

Angie casually notices the odd exchange between friends, as Jon gives Scott a hushing, secretive look. She smiles and leans over to Jon, chiming in on the banter. "Aren't you a bit curious for the story of how Scott escaped?"

Jon glances over at Angie, dejected. "No."

"Really?"

Through roughed-up features, Scott laughs at Angie. "He can always go read the novelized book-version later."

Jon holds his head and peers over at his flippant friend. "Leave me out of it, will you?" Taking a deep calming breath, Jon continues, "Do you realize, not only am I flat busted now, but if you all hadn't come along to pick me up from the ocean, I would be trying to write from some Cuban prison cell?"

With a snort, Scott affirms, "I wouldn't recommend it."

Angie extends a warning finger and wags it at Jon. "That's what you get from chumming-around with Carlos."

Island Stepping with Hemingway

The seaplane bounces through some mild turbulence and Scott, reminiscing, leans over on the vibrating bulkhead. "Some of the places Carlos will take you are not that bad."

Jon looks up at his friend's knowledgeable response. "Speaking from experience, I suppose?"

"Believe me, I've been in worse situations with him." Rollie pokes his head out from the cockpit again and hollers over the engine noise to the passengers in the back. "We'll be swinging around to our home base in a few minutes. Be best if you grab a seat and get buckled up for the landing." The seaplane pilot turns to look at Fulton's rough, banged-up features and laughs jokingly. "Scott... You can do whatever you want back there, since you can't look too much worse." The seaplane continues to rumble across the afternoon sky and banks to the east as the tropical coastline of Key West comes into sight.

XXXIV

Island birds chirp and insects chatter in the lush tropical gardens surrounding the garage apartment. Jon steps out from the doorway and stands at the wrought iron railing to look over the treetops to the view of the street. As he starts to descend the winding stairway, the sounding ring of the antique telephone comes from inside.

A look of dismay flits across his features, and he hesitates a moment before reentering the screened door of the apartment to lift the phone receiver from the ringing cradle. "Hello?"

On the other end of the phone line, the distinct voice of Moselly, prattles on. "Yes, yes, those are exactly the ones that need to be sent over." Annoyed, Jon sighs as the voice continues. "Jonny boy, how are those new pages coming out? I have a few new great ideas for you. Got a minute? Good..."

Jon takes a deep soothing breath and looks out the doorway at the leafy palms and the twisted banyan tree outside. He gingerly eases the old-fashioned telephone receiver from his ear, as his literary agent continues to tediously blather on. Jon glances to his computer on the table, contemplates a moment, then gently sets the receiver on the tabletop and slips out the creaky hinged screen door.

~*~

The midday crowd at the Conch Republic Tavern, consisting mostly of locals is casual and subdued. Despite the musty aroma of spilt beer, dropped cocktails and greasy food, the cool interior of the drinking establishment is a refreshing respite from the humid climate outside. Gangly tan legs in colorful short pants dangle from a high stool, as Casey Kettles sits at the bar with a bottle of energy soda. He swings his legs and swivels on the bar stool as the bar owner approaches.

Angie gives the adolescent boy a playful squeeze on the arm, and he ogles her while tilting down his yellow-rimmed sunglasses. "Angie sweetie, if you weren't old enough to be my mother, I'd take you out on the town."

She smiles and leans on the bar. "What will you do? Take me out *on* the town or *out* of this town?"

The smart-ass kid pulls loose coins from his pocket and slaps them on the bar top. "How far will this get us?"

"Not too far... I ain't that cheap a date."

Casey gives a noticeably antagonizing cough, and the bar owner casts an admonishing gaze to the young customer, "If I was you're mother, you'd get a lot more spankings."

Casey flashes a smiling wink. "That does sound nice!"

Angie rolls her eyes and mutters to the degenerate youth as she walks to the large, round table at the center of the room. "Casey, you need to stop hanging out with Carlos."

Island Stepping with Hemingway

The whole air-sea rescue gang is gathered at the tavern's big round table. Angie sets another pint of beer before Ace as she glances across the table at Rollie, Jon and Fulton. "Anything else I can get you thirsty fellas?" She offers a friendly smile and begins to gather and stack together some of the empty glasses.

Scott Fulton is now dressed in an ivory linen sport suit with a bright tropical-patterned island shirt beneath, mostly unbuttoned. He leans back on the rear legs of the barroom chair and waves a sweeping arm over the table to Angie. "How about another round of drinks for my pals when you get the time, darling?"

The thick glass rim of an empty tumbler clanks as it is stacked into another, and Angie pauses to lift an inquisitive eyebrow toward Fulton. "Who's paying the bill this time?"

"I am, of course. The funds from New York should be wired into my account today. I'll pay off my whole bar tab and Jon's, too."

She cradles a stack of empty glasses to her breast and eyes Fulton with humorous regard. "That same story sounds vaguely familiar from when you were in here last time."

Scott laughs and lets his chair drop back to all fours. "One of these times, surely, it will be true!"

Bemused, Jon stares at the glass of beer on the table in front of him and tilts his head. "I don't think I'll ever get any serious writing done with you hanging around."

Scott takes a long swallow from his garnished mojito cocktail and gestures to the portrait of Hemingway hanging over the bar. "Take it from ol' Papa Hemingway there..." With the stack of empty glasses in her arms, Angie rolls her eyes at Scott while he delivers his lecture on serious writing. "You can't become a serious writer unless you develop and nurture a specific individual fault first." Scott glimpses around the table and raises his cocktail in a toasting fashion. "Now, I choose serious drinking, as my collection of ex-wives has proved to be too expensive for my tastes."

Jon raises his nearly-empty glass, toasting in return. "We always figured the one led to the other."

Rollie laughs, as Jon finishes the remainder of his beverage. "Hey Springer, you seem to have the drinking part down. When do you get to the writing part?"

Angie takes the empty glass from Jon and tucks it under her arm with the others. "And don't forget about the paying part..."

Jon glimpses at Angie beside him as she gives a sultry wink and wriggles her upper torso. He looks across the table to Fulton. "Yeah, Scott, I'll drink to the reimbursement idea."

Kicking his chair back, Scott rises with his practically empty cocktail and takes a broad stance as if to offer another toast. He finishes the drink crunches some ice between his teeth and, with a thud, sets the empty glass down on the table. "I've got to take a piss."

Playful catcalls, hoots and laughter follow Fulton's departure from the table, as he makes a drunken stumble to the restroom at the rear of the tavern. Ace leans back against his chair and observes, as Casey Kettles slips off the high barstool and stealthily ducks out the barroom's side exit door. The mechanic glances over to the tavern's front entrance to see a familiar Key West Detective highlighted in the sunlit entry. "Don't look now, but it appears as if someone informed the local welcoming committee."

XXXV

Inside the Conch Republic Tavern, everyone at the table impulsively turns to the door as Detective Lyle approaches. He stops and stands opposite the table from Angie, letting his stern gaze travel around the assembly of seated suspects. "Hello fellas... And how is everyone this fine afternoon?"

Under his breath, while lifting his beer to take a mouthful, Rollie mumbles, "Were doing fine a minute ago."

The detective turns his stare to the seaplane pilot and narrows an eye knowingly. "I'll have some flight plan issues to discuss with you later. Where's Fulton?"

Ace peers up at the police detective and grumbles, "He's using the toilet and probably having thoughts of you."

Detective Lyle ignores the jabbing remark from the crusty mechanic and turns his officious attentions to Jon. "Was that you *fishing* with Carlos on his boat this morning?"

Jon looks at the blank faces around the table and puts on a friendly smile. "Whatever do you mean officer?"

Shaking his head at the uncooperative gathering, Detective Lyle crosses his arms, heaves his chest and snorts, "What I have to deal with is a Coast Guard helicopter shot to hell and reports of a heavily-armed, probable smuggler vessel near international waters." His gaze travels around the table, studying each person. "A boat that fits the description of a certain yacht was seen to be fleeing the scene of the conflict." The police detective ends on the island newcomer and lifts a pointed finger at him, "I warned you, Springer!"

The clank of empty glass on the bar-top interrupts Lyle's deliberation as Angie unloads an armload of beer mugs. She ambles back to the table and jauntily puts her bar towel to her hip. "What's your business here, Lyle? If you're just going to threaten the tourists, do it at your place, not mine."

Detective Lyle regains his composure and smiles apologetically at Angie. In an effort to implement a different approach with his questioning, the detective takes a breath, and regards Jon. "My apologies, Mister Springer... I was wondering about..."

His hackles suddenly rise again, as he spots Fulton coming from the bathroom. Instantly recognizing the police detective, the troublemaking celebrity hollers across the room, "Hey Lyle, how's life as a *professional dick*?"

The police detective shakes his head at Fulton, unamused at the time-worn wisecrack. "This holiday-making jaunt is over for you, Fulton." Lyle steps around the table. "You're coming in for questioning, and this will hopefully be your last time to my island."

Scott ponders the offer a brief moment then chuckles. "How's my boat? You've been taking care of her for me?"

"It won't be sailing into the sunset anytime soon."

Island Stepping with Hemingway

Fulton lifts a fresh mug of beer from the tabletop and grins before taking a sip. "Probably needs to dry out a bit."

The detective stands beside the table, attempting to control his temper. "You would be wise to do the same."

Scott Fulton stands with a full glass of beer in hand, still smiling at the police detective. He puckers his lips for a kiss and, with two fingertips, taps them in a mocking fashion. "Nope… I have a new lease on life, and I'm gonna live it full."

Jon scoots forward in his chair, leans on the table and looks around the room at his newfound friend then utters, "How was it you were living it before?"

The officer starts to become a bit red under the collar as he stands, glaring, at his rabble-rousing nemesis. Lyle considers Scott Fulton and his celebrity-type an unwelcome sort of tourist. "Fulton, you're in a boatload of trouble already. Come along easy, or I'll have all the boys at the station here to arrest you. It'll be Fantasy Fest '97, all over again."

Jon scoots his chair back to address the police officer. "Detective, why don't you sit down to have a beer with us?" Jon puts on a friendly smile and gestures to an open chair. "We'll tell you the whole story, at least, what we know of it." The detective slowly turns his steely glare to Jon and wobbles his head, warning, "Watch it Bubba, or you'll be next. Hemingway and his celebrity-cronies used this island as a privileged boys' club, but you are not him and your old pal Fulton, there, is no Fitzgerald."

Drinking from the beer mug, Fulton grins wider as he strides toward the detective. "Easy on the literary references there Lyle, or we might think you've read a book or two."

The detective moves a step closer to Scott and offers a pretentious smile. "Are you coming the easy way, Fulton?"

Scott looks down at Jon and the others seated at the table, and then begins to count out loud. "One, two, three…

Eric H. Heisner

When I get to ten, you'll be gone." He takes another gulp from the beer glass as Detective Lyle and the others stare at Fulton, wondering if he's delusional. "Four, five, six..." Scott swirls the handled mug of beer and gives Jon a sly, obvious wink. "Seven, eight..."

With a drunken slur, Fulton utters the number nine, and hauls his free hand back to swing a roundhouse punch that connects with Detective Lyle's jaw. The unprepared officer staggers back and flops against the bar, as Scott raises the remaining brew to his lips, finishing it off. He slams the empty glass mug on the tabletop and looks to Detective Lyle recovering from the blow. "I'm not ready to go anywhere, easy way or not."

Everyone around the table stares in stunned silence, hardly believing what they just witnessed. With his mouth agape, Jon turns to look at Scott, Rollie and Ace, then Angie. "Did he just haul off and hit a police officer?"

Angie nods, making a quick assessment of the valuable breakables around the tavern that might be in the way of the imminent battle. "Yeah... Just like Fantasy Fest '97, all over."

Detective Lyle scoots off the edge of the bar, regains his feet and rubs the sore spot on his jaw while locking infuriated eyes with Fulton. The two opponents stare at each other a second before the police detective grunts and rushes across the room with all the rage of a charging bull. Rollie and Ace grab their drinks, and quickly scoot their chairs back to clear an open path for the contentious adversaries as they make contact. Beverage in hand, Ace grabs Jon by the shirt collar and jerks him aside from his chair. "Best to get clear of this!"

The two combatants tumble back and smash onto the tabletop, as unfinished drinks spill aside. Jon steps away from his fallen chair and the crashing barware, taking in the brawling confrontation. "Holy smokes! Who actually does this outside of saloons in western movies?" The tavern door swings open, casting in a beam of daylight through the entryway as several police officers rush inside. Ace prudently accompanies Jon to the wall, as Rollie finishes off his drink and pushes up his sleeves, ready to get into the action. The old mechanic grunts as the participants of the barroom brawl go crashing across the room, "Step back kid… This sort of thing happens more often than you'd think."

XXXVI

The faint, but steady tapping click of computer keys emits from the upper carriage house apartment. Finally seated at the writing table, Jon lets his fingers dance across the keyboard, filling the screen with lines of words. He pauses a moment to glimpse over to the rotary telephone sitting on the shelf. His fertile mind imagines it ringing again to some new call of adventure, then waits as it sits quietly idle.

There is a creak of the gate hinge at the rear garden entrance, and Jon leans over on the edge of his chair to peer out the front window. He watches the postman sift through a small stack of mail and toss it in a pile, just inside the fence. The distraction from his writing takes hold as Jon turns to the computer screen, poises his fingers over the keypad to type, but lingers. Ultimately, he clicks 'Save' on the document, scoots back his chair and steps outside the apartment to retrieve the mail.

Shortly Jon reenters the garage apartment with the small stack of mail and shuffles through the posted letters. Mumbling to himself aloud, he tosses two of the three aside. "How did they know I'd need one of these credit card loans?" The remaining unopened envelope has an exotic stamp and postmarking as if from some faraway land.

Staring at the thick, cardstock packet with its string closure and wax seal, Jon studies the attractively inscribed handwriting that addresses it to:

Jon T. Springer, Key West - Florida

He studies the envelope and sees that the return address name, just over the sealed closure, reads:

Elizabeth T. Blackwright, Oracabessa Bay - Jamaica

The memory of a long-ago female friendship brings a smile to his face. With a pleasant sigh, he turns the thick envelope over in his hand and murmurs, "What are you up to now, Lizzy?"

Jon is about to break the string and wax seal to open the unusual letter, when the clanking rattle of a bike's chain guard and skidding rubber tires are heard in the street. Jon moves to peek out the window again to see a familiar, long-haired, parrot-toting, bike-riding character near the gate. Letter in hand, he steps out the door to look down at the gardens below.

The distinctive figure of Aston, with the flapping parrot on his shoulder, stands at the gate and offers a broad wave and greeting smile. "Hallo der, Mista Springer. 'Tis a good mornin'." Jon returns a waving hand to the island sage below "Hello, Aston, and a good morning to you."

He watches Aston's colorful bird stretch its wings wide, do a little dancing head bob and two-step, and then tuck them in tight again. Jon puts both hands to the iron railing and calls down. "How is this day treating you, my island friend?"

Island Stepping with Hemingway

"Ah, all da days has da feeling of Saturday for me. And how is it for you dis day?"

Jon looks out from his high-vantage view of the treetops and feels immensely grateful. "It's a fine day for writing stories."

"Dat is good, for dey is always brewing hereabouts." Aston glances back at his decorated bicycle leaning on the fence and up to Jon on the carriage house apartment stoop. "Hey der, da Mista Fulton sent me to fetch you."

"Is he in more trouble?"

"Dis mostly da same trouble, but he wanted to see you 'fore shoving off."

"They're already letting him go?"

Aston waves Jon to come join him at the street level. "Kicked out, or saying let go, is jest a small matter of which side of da gate yer on. Come along now, I'll pedal ya."

Jon looks at the unopened letter and tucks it away in the pocket of his shorts. He peers into the carriage house apartment at his open laptop computer, with the glowing screen, sitting on the table. Uncertain of the hasty invite, he deliberates returning to his writing or seeing-off his troublemaking friend. Muttering to himself under his breath, he defers to the advice from Angie about writing and the magic hat: *"Nothing comes out if you don't put something in first."*

Jon descends the spiral stairway and trots over to Aston by the garden gate "Where is Scott at now?" The shaggy-haired islander grins sagely and gestures over to his highly decorated bicycle leaned up against the wrought-iron fence. "Hop aboard da magic carpet-ride, and I take you to him."

"Really... Again?"

"Yessur... Da Mista Fulton say ta bring dat writer-man to da shipyards on da quick, or he will have to see him in da New York City next time around."

Jon looks down the serene, palm-lined island street, and watches as Aston mounts the banana-styled bicycle seat. In surrender, he drops his chin to his chest and utters to the bearded bicyclist, "Alright. Let's go 'nd see the Mister Fulton." Jon swings a leg over the long seat, and the parrot squawks as Aston spins a pedal and pushes off.

XXXVII

The Historic Key West Marina is its usual busy self, with fishing boats and pleasure yachts of all sizes ready for work. In a whirl of bicycle, bodies and bird wings, Aston delivers his clinging passenger dockside. Jon releases his death-grip hold on the seat of the wheeled contraption parked just in front of Fulton's tethered sailboat, now resting properly in the water.

Dressed in a navy-striped shirt and white linen slacks, Fulton swings through the ship rigging to greet his visitors. He takes a finishing swallow of the drink in his hand and tosses the copper-handled cup aside. "Wow, I didn't think anyone would actually ride on that thing other than Aston."

Jon slides off Aston's two-wheeled ride and is grateful to be on solid ground again. He walks dockside to Fulton at the stern of the recently repaired sailboat. "He told me you were released from lockup and were about to leave?"

"Yeah, Lyle and the other fellas were kind enough to expedite the repairs on my boat hull while I was an honored guest of the Conch Slammer."

"I'm surprised they let you out at all."

Fulton moves to the bow of the sailboat and casts off the dock lines, as Jon follows alongside on the adjoining pier. The roguish grin of his longtime friend flashes as he swings along the ship deck, maneuvering through the sail rigging. "There seems to be nothing that an abundance of well-placed money and a horde of expensive, big city lawyers can't fix."

Jon walks the length of the wooden pier parallel to Fulton on the sailboat deck. He watches as his adventurous friend readies the sailing vessel for departure from the marina. "Speaking of expenses... Have you done that wire transfer of money to pay me back for your ransom?"

Scott unties the line at the stern and tosses the coiled rope to the dock. The boat begins to drift slightly as Scott hoists a sail and spins the ship wheel away from the marina. "Yeah pal, I did have the money set aside for you, but the lawyers ended up using it to get the boat out from impound. I'll have to get you back next time."

Jon stands, dumbstruck, as his absconding friend calmly readies his sailboat and drifts away to open water. "What do you mean, next time?"

Scott beams a wide grin and waves goodbye to Jon. "You'll be just fine. You're a good writer, living in paradise. Write about what you know, or who!"

Jon looks around the crowded marina and almost wishes for Detective Lyle to arrest his impulsive friend and put him in police custody again. Standing dockside, he resists the urge to leap into the water, swim out to the sailboat and climb aboard to throttle Scott. Instead, he cups his hands to his mouth and hollers after the departing ne'er-do-well celebrity.

Island Stepping with Hemingway

"Dang it, Fulton! I'm a penniless writer now, who can't afford to live anywhere!

The Fighting Lady cruises away through the crowded marina, and Scott waves his arm while steering the ship. "That's the making of the best writers. You're welcome!"

Disbelieving, Jon wobbles his head and shrugs-off his friend. He grumbles aloud, as he watches the wind catch the hoisted canvas and the sailboat tilts out toward open sea. "Damn... As usual, when you're the friend of Scott Fulton, you'll be the one to clean the mess and pick up the tab."

Aston stands near his ornate bicycle and beams. "Do ya need a ride to da Conch for a refreshment?"

Jon impulsively nods agreeably to the drink suggestion, then quickly shakes his head as he considers the two-wheeled transportation. "I surely do need that visit to the Conch Tavern, but I think I'll walk this time."

The island sage sweeps back his messy hair and lifts his leg over the curved saddle on the bicycle. He toes the flashy pedals, making them spin in the sunlight, and peels back his overhanging whiskers to form a gracious smile. "Until da next time, writer-man."

Jon offers a thankful wave, as Aston nimbly pedals away with the squawking macaw flapping its vibrant wings. The two-wheeled contrivance veers down the road and turns the corner with a clanking rattle of sparkling accoutrements. The newly destitute adventure author looks out to the gentle ocean waves once again, watching the sun glow through the rising canvas of sailboats on the watery horizon.

Despite familiar memories from earlier times of being in the financial dumps, Jon feels a strange sense of freedom. The exciting sensation of a fresh, newfound life swells inside, brightening his melancholy mood. He looks to the surrounding bustle of the busy marina and breathes in the warm salty air of the tropical island utopia. The sights and sounds of the activity all around fill him with a lust for life as he contemplates a world of creative possibilities.

With a smile, Jon turns on a heel and meanders along the pier. He watches the waterfront birds soaring overhead, diving and fighting over fishmeal scraps. As he walks the street leading toward town, he rounds the corner approaching the avenue enjoyed by the tourists and steers through the sun-kissed multitudes toward the Conch Republic Tavern.

XXXVIII

Entering the musky interior of the Conch Republic Tavern, Jon finally begins to sense the comfortable feelings of home. He steps to the bar and swings his leg over an empty stool. Peering down the rail at the characters bellied-up to the long wooden slab, Jon receives a smile from Angie at the far end. She pulls the ornate handle on a beer tap, finishes the pour and, in Jon's direction, calls down the bar, "Hey there, Springer! Back for more already?"

Jon gives a friendly wave and settles into the cool, sparsely-lit domain of the neighborhood watering hole. Getting situated on the polished seat of the wooden bar stool, Jon feels the bumpy crinkle of something in his pocket and remembers the mysterious letter. He puts a foot to the floor, slips the card-stock envelope from his shorts pocket and smoothes it out across his upper thigh.

Across the polished bar, a bright-eyed Angie appears, glancing inquisitively at the unusual envelope in Jon's hand. "Whatcha got there, Springer? Fan mail find you already?"

Jon looks up and smiles. "Just a letter from a friend."

With her quick eye for detail and a bit of teasing jealousy, Angie eyes the fancy, feminine handwriting as Jon places the envelope on the bar-top. "Well, she must be something of a calligraphy artist, or have a lot of extra time on her hands, to operate an ink pen like that."

Jon peers up at Angie to acknowledge her quick wit and keen insight, as he turns over the envelope to the waxed seal and fastening thread. "She is something of an eccentric when it comes to early traditions, history and lost treasure."

Angie raises a flirting eyebrow, as she watches Jon carefully break the seal and unwind the securing line of string. "So broke that you're already looking for lost treasure, huh? Didn't you already have enough with pirates this week?"

Jon grunts affirmative as he opens the envelope and slides a folded note from inside. He reads it silently and then looks across to Angie, who waits with mounting curiosity. She smiles amiably at Jon, leans forward and puts her hands to the edge of the bar. "So, is it good news or bad news?"

Jon places the unfolded note on the wooden bar surface and turns its orientation for Angie to read. While he empties the envelope of its remaining contents, Angie peers down at the letter and quietly reads the short message:

Jon, I need your help... Please come to Jamaica at your earliest convenience. Bring the map, a change of clothes and your eye for detail.

-with love, Lizzy

Island Stepping with Hemingway

From the envelope, Jon slowly removes an old wax-paper map with the outline of an island and an inset of the north-east coastline. An inked 'X' marks the spot of some mysterious location. Jon glimpses up to meet Angie's gaze. He spreads the paper out on the bar between them and whispers, "This looks to be a treasure map…"

Angie smiles and nods her head. "Yes, it surely does." She takes a bottle of Blackwell Rum from the back bar, grabs two glasses and sets them both up with a generous pour. Sliding the tumbler to Jon, she lifts hers in a toasting fashion. "Cheers to a new and exciting tomorrow, and to the untold mysteries of these islands."

Jon lifts his stout glass to clink with hers and downs the sweet, dark liquor. He feels the warming sensation of rum pulsate through his body, then realizes the cold chill of reality. "I can't afford the travel to Jamaica!"

"Why not?"

"I spent my last dime on Scott's ransom demand."

Angie lifts her foot onto something under the bar, downs the full rum shot and puts her hand to her raised knee. She smiles across the wooden surface to Jon and gestures at the old payphone hung on the wall near the end of the bar. "All I have to do is call in a favor from Rollie, and you'll have first class airfare to the island of Jamaica."

Angie sets her tumbler down on the bar with a thud and beams a knowing grin. "It's not every day that you get a handwritten invitation to adventure."

Jon looks down at the old parchment paper map and over to the handwritten note requesting his help. "When am I getting any writing done?"

Angie pours them another shot of rum and sets the bottle aside. "Some folks just want to make a living and others choose to make a life. The writing will come after you get some real-life living in."

Jon lifts the glass of dark rum from the bar surface, looks at the beautiful saloon keeper standing across from him and lets the contents of the glass glimmer in the dim tavern lighting. "That is… if I survive."

The End

I allow myself to be understood as a colorful fragment in a drab world.

\-   Errol Flynn

The author in the Florida Keys - 1999

Eric H. Heisner is an award-winning writer, actor and filmmaker. He is the author of several Western and Adventure novels: *West to Bravo, Seven Fingers a' Brazos, T. H. Elkman, Africa Tusk* and *Wings of the Pirate*. He can be contacted at his website:

www.leandogproductions.com

Emily Jean Mitchell is an artist, teacher and mother who enjoys spending time in the garden and outdoor playtime with her husband, son and dog in Austin, Texas.

www.mlemitchellart.com

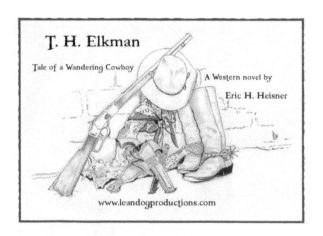

CPSIA information can be obtained
at www.ICGtesting.com
Printed in the USA
LVHW041202280419
615848LV00006B/28